MW01104607

Barcelona

Jones

Murder on Broadway

Barcelona Jones is a Broadway star. Her new play, *Murder on Broadway* is a big hit with people waiting months to buy a ticket to see it.

At one evening performance, at the end of the first act, real bullets are put into the prop gun killing one of the cast players. Were the bullets meant for him or one of the other players?

Soon, another murder occurs, as well as two attempted murders: one of them on the star, Barcelona Jones herself.

Barcelona hires a private detective to investigate the crimes, and he completely falls in love with her on their first meeting.

Will her feelings for Sam, the detective, be the same? And who is the murderer? Could it possibly be Barcelona's friend and stage actress, Brenda Summers? That's up to you, the reader, to find out.

Barcelona Jones

Jones

Murder on Broadway

by

Chuck Antone, Jr.

© 2014 Chuck Antone, Jr.

ISBN 13: 978-1-4949-6945-5

Direct Scripture quotations are taken from
the NEW AMERICAN STANDARD BIBLE®
Copyright © 1960,1962,1963,1968,1971,1972,1973,1975,1977,1995
by The Lockman Foundation. Used by permission.

HEARTEN PUBLISHING
P.O. Box 4404
Kailua-Kona, HI 96745
United States of America

antoneyboksu@gmail.com

Dedication

To Doni, my wife of sixty great years as of this writing. How many more will the Lord graciously give to us?

While writing *Barcelona Jones* I reminisced a lot about how we met and how I knew you were the one I was going to marry, even tho' you were not my date that April night in 1953.

When I told my mother and father that I had found the girl I was going to marry, my mother responded just as Sam's mother did in *Barcelona Jones*, "How do you know? You haven't even kissed her yet." A lot of the characteristics of Sam and Barcelona Jones comes from us.

We were both so young, but praise God, when He puts something together it lasts forever.

I LOVE M.B.W. . . . FROM Y.F.P.

Acknowledgements

As always to my wife, Doni, for the many proof readings and suggestions . . . plus her patience.

To Chris, my editor, who has been a blessing to me. This is our fifth book together. Each one gets better and better because of you. Many thanks, and may Jesus bless you, my friend, each day.

More Books by Chuck Antone, Jr.

Lord, Send Me

The author's feelings and emotions while facing a one year prison sentence in a third world country.

Available in English or Chinese.

Dear Peter, Love Chuck

A letter to the apostle Peter on how he has encouraged the author to walk closer to Christ.

In bilingual, English and Chinese

The Centurion and the Crown of Thorns

A fictional story about the Centurion who, at the foot of the cross, said, "Truly this was the Son of God."

As people leave the scene of the crucifixion, the Centurion, known in this book as Marcus, stays a little longer. While he's looking up at Jesus who is still nailed to the cross beams, a small earthquake happens. The crown of thorns falls off Jesus' head and rolls to the feet of Marcus, where it stops.

As Marcus bends down and touches the crown he senses a strong power coming from it. He immediately feels clean and new, and a great peace comes over him. He doesn't understand it but he enjoys the feeling.

He takes the crown home to share his story with his wife, who wants nothing to do with it. After all, she was one of the many who were in the courtyard yelling for Jesus to be crucified. On the other hand, his ten-year-old son is fascinated by what his father tells him, and is intrigued by the crown and wants to learn more.

Marcus and his son Antony become believers, and Marcus searches out ten Bible prophecies that Jesus has fulfilled. He wants to teach his son many things about their new Messiah.

The crown not only gives Marcus strength and peace, but it also has healing powers that bring him and his son Antony closer in their walk with the Lord.

As the story unfolds, Marcus learns how each of the ten prophecies was fulfilled. And because of this, he is now ready to completely give his life to his new God, especially after he has an opportunity to meet with the risen Jesus face to face, who tells him it is time to give up the crown of thorns.

You've Got to be Kidding, Lord, with the subtitle – You want me to tell *who* about You?

Share the Gospel? Does the thought make you want to hide in bed with the blankets over your head? If it does, you're not alone, but help is at hand. Here is what Chuck Antone, Jr. says in this exciting book written with great humor and much understanding:

"Are you ready to experience sharing Christ with the lost? Does one name keep popping into your mind? Has God been whispering in your ear? If so, be challenged, make that contact and see what God can do.

"Be encouraged by just being available. Just be the instrument, the tool. Let God do the work. He is much better at it than we are, for He has had a lot more experience in bringing someone to His Son, Jesus Christ. After all, He is God, the Mighty One, the Powerful One, the Creator, Our Savior, Our Father, the One and Only God."

ISBN 978-1-9350-7934-7

神呀！你沒開玩笑吧你...
要我向他傳福音嗎？

You've Got to be Kidding, Lord

in Chinese
ISBN 978-1-4818-2238-1

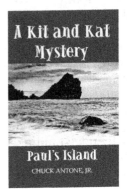

Paul's Island

Volume 1. A Kit and Kat mystery. Fiction. A mystery about eight university graduates who spend five days on the island. When one of them is murdered, the others help the Inspector solve the case. The two main characters are Christians with criminology degrees.
ISBN 978-0-6154-7577-6

High Seas Murder

Volume 2. A Kit and Kat mystery. Fiction. Kit and Kat have just set up their own private detective agency, and are ready to go on a Mediterranean cruise before they open up their doors for business. The cruise is meant to be a time of relaxation, but the onboard theft of a necklace worth over $3,000,000 needs their investigative skills. Soon it's not just stolen jewelry that Kit and Kat are involved with, as theft turns to murder on the High Seas.
ISBN 978-1-4681-2356-2

Ava Montez – Her Life and Death

Fiction. Who killed Hollywood legend Ava Montez, once known as the most beautiful woman in the world? The murder has been unsolved for over forty years. But that's about to change, when the *New York Reader's* reporter, Rae Collins, is assigned to do a story on the life and death of Ava Montez.

The murderer, who has felt safe all these years, is now threatened by Rae's interviews with the four original suspects. And she's already getting too close. The only way to prevent being caught and sent to prison for life is to murder again. And Rae is to be the murderer's next victim! ISBN 978-0-6154-4522-9

Barsabbas

Fictional love story between a man and a woman, and their love for Jesus, as He teaches them from the book of Mark.
ISBN 978-1-6157-9058-6

For order form and information on books and CDs:

P.O. Box 4404
Kailua-Kona, HI 96745
United States of America

Email: antoneyboksu@gmail.com

About the Author

Chuck and Doni have been missionaries since 1981. They live on the Big Island of Hawaii.

They have two children, four grandchildren and four great grandchildren.

They have helped start churches in the Philippines, Hong Kong, So. Africa and also Taiwan where Chuck ministers four months each year.

They have also done outreaches in Japan, Indonesia and in the mainland USA. They have smuggled Bibles into mainland China and have hiked up mountains in the Philippines while being watched by the New Peoples' Army, a Communist group that lives and hides in the mountain areas.

Chuck was also arrested in a third world country and faced a year in prison for teaching a seminar on how to be a witness for Christ. After three weeks he was deported and sent back to his home in Hawaii.

He says, "Being a Christian is only boring when one makes it be boring."

Chuck is the Pastor of the Kona Coast Chaplaincy on the Big Island of Hawaii, and he along with Doni are the Directors of Go Spread His Word Ministries, Inc. founded in 1990.

You can contact Chuck at:
antoneyboksu@gmail.com
or write
P.O. Box 4404, Kailua-Kona, HI 96745

Chuck's books can also be purchased through major Internet sellers.

Chapter One

Tuesday

When anyone hears I'm married to Barcelona Jones, the questions begin:

"How did you meet her?"

"When did you fall in love with her?"

"How long have you been married to her?"

And of course the statement that I've heard so often, "You sure are a lucky guy."

I don't think there's a soul living on this planet that hasn't heard of Barcelona Jones. And they all seem to be madly in love with her.

Tonight Barcelona and I are celebrating our fiftieth wedding anniversary. Time has flown by so fast.

I'll be with her in just over an hour. Our three children will also be with us.

So while I'm getting ready, let me take you back a little over fifty years to the 1960s, and tell you the story of how I met and fell in love with Barcelona Jones, stage and screen actress.

It was on a rainy evening when I left my office. I was at that time a private detective, just as my father was. When he decided to retire he asked me to take over the business. I'd been preparing for it for a long time. By his encouragement I went to college and received my degree in criminology. I also studied some law as I believed it would help me. I knew it would be important while investigating the many cases I had, for protection of me and my clients.

Our daughter Lisbon now runs the agency and she's very good at it. She also holds a degree in criminology.

I was being trained by Dad while going to school. And after I graduated we worked side by side for almost six years. When he thought I was ready to take over, he retired and left it all to me. For over thirty years he'd built the business into a very successful and well known agency. His words to me were, "Sam my son, you're ready. I have no second thoughts. Your mom and I are going to enjoy our remaining years together."

My home was just a little over two miles from my office, so most of the time I walked. But that night because of the rain I looked for a taxi. I saw one parked across the street, so I ran over and got in the cab just about the same time as Barcelona did through the opposite door.

She smiled and said, "Oh, I'm sorry. I thought this was my cab. I had called for one," while putting her hand on the door handle ready to get out.

I said, "No, it's me who's sorry. I thought it was available and just got in. I'm sure it must be your cab."

"It's okay, I'm not going very far. Just to the Shuster Theater. We can share if you like. It's a terrible day with the rain and wind. No one should be walking in it."

"That would be great. The theater is right on my

way. I walk past it most every day, but on the other side of the street. Sharing would be fine, if you don't mind." I paused for a moment, then stretching out my hand I said, "Hi, I'm Sam."

"Hello, I'm Barcelona," looking up at me. For a second I thought she was expecting some kind of a reaction. I wasn't sure why, so I said, "Barcelona? That's an interesting name. How did you come by it?"

Flashing that wonderful smile of hers, all she said was, "My parents had their reasons."

As we rode the short distance in silence, I took in her features: the blonde hair, her eyes, and of course the face. I was thinking she was beautiful enough to be a movie star. Little did I know who she really was.

When we arrived at her destination she reached into her bag to pay the fare.

I said, "Please let me get it. After all, this is your taxi and you have graciously let me ride in it. That's the least I can do. Please, I insist."

"All right, since you insist. But here take these two tickets. It's for the performance tonight at this theater. Bring a date, a wife, fiancée or a friend."

"A friend I can bring. Don't have a wife or a fiancée. Thanks. I was wondering what I was going to do tonight. Will I be seeing you there?"

"Yes, I'll be there." She got out of the taxi, turned to me gave me that dazzling smile of hers, and a look as if I was missing something.

Chapter Two

At that time I was not much on theater plays, so I knew little about them. My thing at that time – remember, it was over fifty years ago – was watching a good movie either on TV or at one of our movie houses. But since I had two free tickets in the palm of my hand when I got home, I called my sister Erica who was always talking about one of the many plays she and her husband Rick had seen.

I knew that if she hadn't seen this one, whatever it was and if it had good reviews, she would want to go if she had no other plans for the evening. Besides, Rick was off someplace on a business journey, and she was all alone because my mom had taken their kids for a few days. Don't get me wrong: they had and have a great marriage and have two adorable children, and I love being called Uncle Sam even these many years later. Rick and I have always been good friends. He met my sister on a double date that I had arranged.

"Hi sis, what are your plans for this evening?" I had called her just as soon as I got home.

"Nothing much. I'm on call at the hospital, the midnight shift, and it's quiet here without Rick and the kids. So I'm just catching up on some long-delayed projects. Why? What's up?"

"Well, I know how much you love the theater, and

someone gave me two free tickets for a play for tonight. I'm wondering if you'd like to go with me – if you haven't already seen it."

"Oh, you can't find a date, huh?"

"Actually you're the first one I called. I know how much you love the theater."

"What's the play?"

"Not sure."

"Well, look on the ticket. It should say."

I remember fumbling for the ticket and when I found it I read aloud, "*Murder on Broadway.* Have you heard about it?"

"You've got to be kidding. That's a hot show. Are you sure it's for tonight? It takes over six months to get a ticket for that play. I think someone's playing a joke on you. Are you sure it wasn't for last night's performance?"

I looked at the date. "No, the date on the ticket is definitely for tonight. It must be a good play then?"

"Yes it is. Right now it's the number one show on Broadway. Who gave you the ticket?"

"Some knock-out blonde I met in a taxi this evening on the way home. She had a real odd name … Barcelona." Then laughing, I said, "I wonder if her last name is Spain!"

Erica ignored my remark and asked, "Barcelona? Doesn't that name mean anything to you, Sam?"

"Nope, but you've got to admit it is a little strange. So will you go with me or not?"

"Of course. I wouldn't miss it for the world. Even if I was in the middle of an operation I'd drop everything. Not only to see the play, but to see the look on your face."

I knew of course that Erica was just kidding. She

was a great doctor and surgeon at St. Ann's Hospital. In my opinion the best, I may add. The whole family was very proud of her. I wanted to ask her what she meant by the look on my face, but she quickly asked what time and where we should meet.

"Well, since you live further out, you get a taxi and come by and pick me up. The performance starts at eight, so how about being here at 7:30? I'll be waiting outside of my building."

"Good. See you then. And, Sam, remember this is a dressy affair. Not tux night, but a nice suit would be good."

"What, no shorts and tee shirts tonight? I'll try and look my best. I wouldn't want to embarrass you."

Right on schedule Erica showed up. It was still raining and with the help of the doorman holding an umbrella over my head, I managed to join her in the taxi without getting too wet, because the rain had turned to a gentle mist.

"You look very handsome tonight, Sam. I'm going to hang on to your arm and make all of the single girls there jealous."

"Thanks, Sis. You as always look smashing."

When we arrived at the theater I got out first, then reached back and helped Erica out. She had this big mischievous smile on her face. She looked up and with her finger pointed to the marquee. I looked up and in big letters was *Murder on Broadway*. In even larger and bolder letters, I read, **STARRING BARCELONA JONES.**

7

Chapter Three

After looking up and seeing who the star was, I turned to Erica. She gave out this big laugh and said, "I can't believe you pass by here every day and never noticed the name Barcelona on the marquee."

I shrugged my shoulders, put on my best sheepish look and said, "I walk across the street and have other things on my mind. Besides, you know what I think of Broadway plays. Too costly and too formal."

I remember we both walked in, arm and arm. The usher gave us a program and led us to our seats. Erica looked over at me and whispered, "You probably don't realize it, but these are great seats given to you by the star who is a great actress and has had many good reviews."

Soon the theater got dark. Silence fell upon the audience and *Murder on Broadway* began.

After five minutes, Barcelona entered. The applause was thunderous to my ears. All of the actors on stage froze in their positions. When the applause quieted down, the actors came back into the characters they were playing. It was truly amazing.

Barcelona was spellbinding. My heart kept skipping beats every time she spoke or was just on the stage. Something deep inside of me kept telling me that I wasn't only *falling* in love with Barcelona Jones, but I *was* in love with her.

I know it may sound strange and you may be saying, "Impossible." But you are so wrong. It *is* possible and I am living proof. Do I believe in love at first sight? A few hours before, I might have said, "No way." But now after experiencing it, I have to say, "Yes way!" Has this ever happened to you?

The end of the first act was coming to a close. As the actors stood on the stage, the scene was celebrating a birthday. One of the players pulls out a gun and shoots the leading male star. Everyone on the set screams. The actor who was shot falls to the floor and the curtain comes down. The applause begins.

It was so loud that at first we couldn't hear the panic voice of Barcelona, "*He's really been shot. He really has been shot.*"

Most of us there started to look at each other thinking it was still part of the play. Then Barcelona appeared between the two drawn curtains and with a very shaky voice asked, "Is there a doctor in the house? Mr. Sparks has *really* been shot. He's bleeding."

"I'm a doctor, please let me through." Erica by now was trying to get through the crowd and I was following close behind her. The curtains were parted a little. We went through them and the male star was lying on the floor in a small pool of blood.

Erica leaned over the body. She looked over at me, shook her head, then announced to everyone on the stage, "I believe this man has expired. Please, no one touch anything, and wait for the police to arrive."

The actors standing around were shuffling their feet. I was noticing different emotions on their faces, most of them looks of unbelief.

I told everyone to stay where they were, then asked Erica to call the police and to tell them a homicide had taken place at the Shuster Theater. Of course the word given back was that no one was to leave the building. Within fifteen minutes the Chief Inspector arrived to ask questions.

I turned to see what Barcelona was doing. She looked scared, bewilderment on her face. I wanted to go over and put my arms around her. After all, wasn't that what people did when they were in love with a person who seems to be confused and almost in tears? Then I remembered that at least for now this was a one-sided love affair. Besides, she gave no recognition that she even knew who I was.

When the police arrived, Chief Inspector Martin (Marty) Mead, an old friend of my parents and also a friend of mine, walked up on the stage. The curtains were now fully closed. My father and Marty had worked on many cases together and had become very good friends. Marty and I had worked on only a few.

He looked over at me and smiled. "Hi Sam. Nice seeing you. Are you on this case?"

"No, I was in the audience when Miss Jones——" I looked over at her to see if by now maybe she recognized me. But no ... nothing. I continued on, "Miss Jones called for a doctor, and my sister Erica went up to see what she could do."

The Chief looked over at Erica and gave her a nod of recognition. After all, he had known both of us since we were teenagers when he and Dad started to work together.

Then he looked over at me. "Sam, since you're not on the case I'm going to have to ask you to give your statement and then leave. Erica, you can give me a short statement, then you'll be able to leave with Sam." Then he turned to the cast members. "The rest of you take a seat. We'll be asking all of you some questions, and we may be here for a long time."

I wanted to stay but knew the Chief was right. Unless I was hired for the job, or was one of the actors and crew, I had no business being there. I looked back at Barcelona. Still nothing. Not even one of her smiles.

Chapter Four

Erica wasn't ready to go home, so we walked back to my place for a nightcap. The rain had stopped and the stars were trying to peek through the clouds. Our nightcap consisted of hot fudge Sundays and decaf coffee. It was always available at my condo, and still is at Barcelona's and my home.

Erica had about an hour before having to check in at the hospital, where she always kept a change of clothes. This meant she could go right from my place to the hospital.

We talked about the murder, the show, and of course Barcelona. When we'd left, people were standing in line for their refunds. We'd been told that the play was sold out for the next six months, so the theater could not guarantee a seat any time soon. Erica and I just walked out. After all, our tickets had been free.

As Erica was leaving my apartment, I mentioned that I wished I was on the case and that I would have loved to get to know the star more. My sister gave me that mischievous smile again. I had a feeling she knew I'd fallen for Barcelona. She didn't have to say anything. The look was enough. And I had seen that know-it-all look many times before.

I tossed and turned all night. I knew that one of the suspects would be the person who fired the shot. But that seemed too easy. So I was wondering who might have put real bullets in the gun. And of course, why?

Real bullets. Something bothered me there, but I couldn't think what. I was thinking about motive. Maybe the understudy wanted a chance for stardom. I'd read a book about such a thing when I was a kid. That's a detective's mind, always looking and searching for a new clue that no one else had figured out yet.

Intermingling through all of this were, of course, my feelings for Barcelona. Was she engaged? Maybe even married? Or did she have a steady boy friend? I thought I would ask my sister. She would know, because she kept up on all of this entertainment business. I was also wondering where I would figure in all of this, or even if I would.

One thing I knew: I wasn't going to give up. I even dreamt of our wedding day and Barcelona all in white walking down the aisle. But before I could say, "I do," I woke up and started the whole process of Barcelona, the wedding, and the murder all over again.

I finally got up, showered and had a bowl of Cheerios, got dressed and walked to the office. The rain had stopped and the air was cool and brisk. It was just the way I liked it when walking to and from the job.

Chapter Five

Wednesday

I arrived at the office about 7:15 a.m. Donna, my secretary, came in at 8:45 sharp, as she did each day. She had worked for the firm for over twenty-five years, and started when she was twenty-five. When my dad retired Donna asked me if she could still stay on, because she loved her job. Of course I said yes, as I had no intentions of letting her go.

My dad always said Donna was a great asset to our agency. He'd told me I'd be wise to keep her on, but no pressure. He also said that the place was mine and to do what I felt was best for the business.

Donna was one of those God-sent people: easy to get along with, smart as whip, and as Dad said, valuable to our company.

At 9:45 Donna called me on the intercom. "There's a woman here who would like to see you."

"Does she have an appointment? I don't have anyone down for 9:45."

"No." Then in a very quiet whisper, "You'd be foolish not to see her. She's a knockout."

A knockout! I was wondering, could it possibly be Barcelona Jones? She was the only knockout I would be interested in.

"Okay, Donna, send her in."

I waited, holding my breath. The door knob turned and in walked Barcelona Jones. My heart started to skip beats again. Even through the dark glasses and the hat hiding part of her face, I couldn't help recognizing her. I remember I jumped up so quickly that my chair rolled towards the window behind my desk and crashed against the wall. The Boston fern wobbled back and forth in its plant stand, almost falling over. I held my breath until it stopped.

I felt flustered, and as I walked around my desk I hit my thigh on its corner. I wanted to shout out, "Ouch," but kept my lips tight. I reached out to shake her hand, but instead motioned for her to sit down in one of the two chairs facing my desk. I felt like a complete idiot.

She gave me that amazing smile as she sat down. Removing her hat and glasses, she said, "Hi Sam, in case you have forgotten, I'm Barcelona Jones." She paused for a moment, "We met last night in the taxi."

You can probably guess by now that those words melted me away in an instant. She remembered me, she remembered me, was all I kept thinking.

"Of course, Miss, or is it Mrs. Jones?"

"It's Miss Jones, but please call me Barcelona." Then looking me straight in the eyes, and with a little grin, she said, "We're practically old friends."

Old friends. I liked that, but sweethearts would have been better.

I came to my senses quickly. "Barcelona..." I loved saying that name. "... Barcelona, why do I have this honor of you gracing my office?"

Just as soon as I said it, I thought: *How stupid. Get a hold of yourself. Be professional. She apparently came here to hire you.* So I covered up by saying, "Before the tragedy happened last night you were marvelous. You had us all captivated. My sister says you're up for an Emmy. She keeps up on these things. As for me, I love a good movie."

I felt my face turning red, another foot-in-the-mouth episode.

"Thank you, but I think your sister most likely said that I was nominated for a *Tony* award. The Emmy is a TV award, and, Sam, believe it or not I also like a good movie."

"Yes, of course it was a Tony. I remember now." I'm sure my face was still red.

"It's all right, Sam, many people get them mixed up. I came here, as you can probably guess, because of the murder last night. I saw you there, and after you left I asked the Chief about you. He said you're one of the best detectives in the city. So I asked him for your address. He happily gave it to me and said he enjoys working with you. I couldn't sleep all night just thinking about it and wondering who would want to kill Anthony Sparks."

"Yes, I was up all night myself thinking about the murder also and about——" This time I stopped myself. I wasn't about to say, "And you."

Instead, I said, "I thought maybe the murderer could be an understudy, a director or one of the producers wanting to sell more tickets to the play. I'm sure more people will want to buy them now. I can just see the headlines in the paper: *Murder on Broadway* becomes a reality."

"No, I'm sure it's not the director or one of the producers. There's no reason for them to have murdered *anyone*. The show is already a big hit and it's sold out for at least the next six months. My contract is for another year, and praise God it's a wonderful hit. Of course more people will want to see it, and I'm sure at the end of scene one, when the audience hears the shots they'll wonder if they'll be witnessing another murder."

"What about the stand-in. Who is he? Maybe he wants a chance to play in such a big hit on Broadway."

"No again, Sam. The dead man *is* the stand-in. John Ashland, the lead actor, called in sick at the last minute. He was rushed to the hospital. He had to have his stomach pumped and was given medication. I called him this morning. He's under observation and hoping to be released this afternoon. He'll be performing tonight. I'm sure you've heard the saying, 'The show must go on.'

"He's allergic to all kinds of peanut products. He must have eaten something yesterday, not realizing there was some kind of peanut extract in the food. He's always very careful. In the last two months this is the third time this has happened. But this was the first time he's missed a performance.

"The reason why I'm here is because I think that whoever the killer is, meant to have John Ashland murdered instead of Anthony Sparks. Somehow real bullets were put in the gun last night, but I'm not sure how that was done. The prop man told the Chief he'd put the blanks in two hours before the show was to go on, as he does every night. He doesn't like to wait for the last minute. He's a good guy and has been a prop man for some of my other plays. He himself has no motive to kill anyone that I can think of."

"How many people knew about Mr. Ashland being allergic to this peanut stuff?" I asked.

"Just about everyone. John Ashland always makes

sure all the actors and other people involved in a play he's doing knows. He takes no chances, and is a great actor. This is the second time I've worked with him."

"If he's so great, why did the writers want to kill him off in the first act?"

"They didn't. The next scene was to take place in the hospital. The character recovers and continues on being the villain, but all the audience wishes he *had* died. That's how bad the character is that he plays, and he's very good at it."

"Well, it looks like someone nearly had their wish fulfilled, but they got the wrong man. I'll take on the case. And as a favor to you, no charge."

Barcelona shook her head in protest and started to speak.

"No, please let me do this," I said. Then I used the same words that I had used the night before in the taxi, "I insist."

With a twinkle in her eyes she said, "Okay, Sam, if you insist." She reached into her purse and took out two more tickets, "These are for tomorrow night's performance. Please bring your sister Erica again. I'd like to meet her properly. She's very beautiful."

"Yes, she is. At school we were known as Beauty and the Beast!"

As she handed me the tickets, she smiled. "I'm sure they were only kidding."

I took the tickets, looked at them, and then started to hand them back. She must have read my mind.

Very sweetly she said, "I'm the star you know. They give me a few free tickets for each performance to give to my friends. It's part of my contract."

I was in seventh heaven. She called me her friend. Well at least that's the way I took it.

Chapter Six

I asked Barcelona, "Do you think it will be possible for us to go and visit the actor who has the peanut allergy? John Ashland, isn't it? I'd like to ask him a few questions."

"Yes, I'm sure it will be. But first let me call him to make sure. May I use your phone?"

"Of course."

I stood and handed her the receiver. I intentionally touched her hand but made it look like an accident. I wanted to see her reaction – there wasn't one.

She exchanged a few words with the actor, then turned to me. "Yes, we can go. John says he'd love to have visitors. He's bored, but happy. He'll be released from the hospital at three this afternoon, so we will have plenty of time to see him. I'll meet you there, say in about an hour and a half? I have some things I have to take care of first."

"What hospital is he in?"

"Saint Ann's. It's not too far from here."

"Okay, I know it well. It's the hospital my sister Erica is assigned to."

"Will she be there? Maybe I'll be able to meet her if she is."

"Not sure. She was on call at midnight last night. She may still be there, and if she is you can meet her. If not, then tomorrow night at the theater."

Barcelona left. To say I was disappointed that we wouldn't be riding in a taxi together to the hospital, is an understatement. But I was going to see her again, and besides, I did get to hold her hand. Even if it was just for a moment. That was when she was leaving as I shook it and told her goodbye.

Chapter Seven

Barcelona and I arrived at St. Ann's hospital at the same time. I quickly jumped out of my taxi and ran over to hers to open the door and reach for her hand which she graciously extended into mine. As I guided her out of the taxi, I was in seventh heaven again. Of course my heart was doing those strange things. I was falling hopelessly in love.

As we walked down the hall, one of the nurses said, "Hi Sam. Erica said you'd be here today. You just missed her. She said you'd be in to question the guy in room 409. When I asked her how she knew, she said it was her detective instinct, whatever that means. I thought *you* were the detective?"

"Correct you are, but remember Erica was raised in a detective family. Is it all right for us to go in?"

"Yes, he's getting ready to leave, even though he still has a few hours to go."

We took the elevator up to the fourth floor and entered the actor's room.

John Ashland was sitting on the bed completely clothed and looking ready to leave the facility as soon as he was given the okay. He looked a little pale and shaken by what had happened to him.

Barcelona made an introduction, saying that she

had "hired me" to investigate the case. She told him she thought that the murderer actually wanted him killed instead of the understudy that night, Anthony Sparks.

"No way. Why would anyone want to kill *me*? I don't have any enemies."

Barcelona agreed. "I'm sure you don't. But, John, to make me feel good, please answer the questions that Sam will ask you."

"Okay, detective Sam, fire away. I want Barcelona to feel good." After saying that, he gave a little chuckle.

"I'm wondering, did you spend a long time with anyone yesterday?"

"I had lunch with Mike, my agent." He looked over at Barcelona and smiled. "Mike said I was up for the movie part to play Billy the bully in the movie of *Murder on Broadway*. He said that there were three others besides me being considered."

I broke in, "Did he happen to mention who the other three were?"

"Yes, I guess it's no secret. Besides myself, there's another Broadway actor, Peter Holmes. I think you've worked with him before, Barcelona. Is that right?"

Barcelona nodded. "Two plays back. He was very good as I recall. He wasn't the lead actor, but received very good reviews."

"Quite a handsome guy, I believe. The other possibility for the movie is Charlie Long, who I understand is very hot in Hollywood right now. His last two pictures I hear have made big bucks. The last one is, or rather was, Anthony Sparks, who of course is now no longer a contender."

Turning to me, Ashland asked, "Do you think that

it's possible that the killer tried to kill me last night instead of Anthony Sparks?"

"It's possible, but maybe not only *you*, knowing you're allergic to peanuts, but Anthony Sparks at the same time."

Barcelona turned to me, frowning. "How could someone kill John here, *and* Anthony Sparks, with a single bullet?"

"It could be like this," I explained. "Maybe the killer thought if he gave John enough peanut extract, it would kill him. So the killer could get two birds in one night." I looked at John, watching his face carefully. "Is there a possibility someone could have dosed your food with peanut oil without you knowing?"

"I suppose so. The doctors have told me that even a small amount could be life threatening if I wasn't careful. So you think that perhaps the killer tried to get rid of *both* of us yesterday, but only succeeded with Anthony?"

"It's possible. I'm not saying it's a sure thing, but it could be. Tell me, how long have you had this Mike as your agent?"

"A long time. He's a go-getter. That's why I made the change many years ago. My other agent didn't do too much. I was the one who had to hustle to get the good parts."

"Would Mike gain anything to see you dead?"

"You've got to be kidding. I can't see why he'd want to lose his commission. He also handles Peter Holmes, one of the other three contenders for the Hollywood part."

I looked over at Barcelona. "How about you? Are you up for the starring role in the movie?"

"Yes," she replied, with what I thought was a slight blush. "Although it's not been made public yet, I've already been given the roll. I've even signed the contract."

"Congratulations." Both John Ashland and I said it at the same time.

On the way out of the hospital, I asked Barcelona if she had any time off during the show's run.

She said, "My contract reads that I'm to have every Wednesday off, as long as the show runs. As you know, today is Wednesday, my free day. The theater is closed today. Why do you ask? Does it have something to do with the case?"

"I'm not sure."

I was thinking how fortunate it was for John Ashland that he had all day to rest, and half of tomorrow before he had to perform.

"May I ask you a question now, Sam?"

"Yes, fire away."

"Well, Sam, you've never told me your last name. You do have one, don't you?"

Without thinking, I again put my foot in my mouth. "Let's just say that if we ever got married you wouldn't have to change your name."

Her cheeks got a little flushed. I could have kicked myself for making her feel uncomfortable. But she recovered well.

"Are you kidding me, Sam? Is your last name Jones?" Then with a frivolous laugh she repeated my name, "Sam. Sam Jones. I love it."

I wanted to respond "I love *you*, Barcelona Jones."

Chapter Eight

Leaving the hospital, Barcelona and I took the first taxi in a line of six that were waiting for passengers. I opened the door for her and gently helped her in, then ran over to the other side and joined her in the back seat. We both laughed, as it reminded us of our first meeting which was only the day before, but seemed much longer. I was thinking that in less than twenty-four hours I had fallen madly in love with one of the most famous stars on Broadway.

I decided to take the plunge. "Barcelona, since today is Wednesday, and if you're free tonight, would you consider having dinner with me?"

She hesitated. I held my breath. My heart was not skipping any beats. This time it felt like it had completely stopped.

"I'm sorry, Sam, but I'm not ready for a relationship just yet. I like you. You're sweet, congenial and very handsome. But at the moment I'm just concentrating on my career here in New York, and sometime next year in Hollywood to make the movie. It's a great opportunity for me. Part of me wants to say yes to your dinner invitation, and another part of me says no. My philosophy has always been, when in doubt, don't."

"I understand, but what if we made it a business meeting. I still have some questions I'd like to ask about the murder, and about the men up for the movie roll. It will be strictly a dinner between the client and the agency. I feel like it may all be connected somehow."

"Oh, Sam, you're making it more difficult for me." She smiled while she said this, and my heart started to beat again. "Let me think about it. I'll call you in an hour. Is that okay with you?"

"Well, it's better than a quick no." This time I had a smile on my face.

I dropped her off at the place she was staying, and gave the taxi driver the instructions to my office where Donna was waiting for me. She said that Chief Mead wanted me to call him as soon as I got to the office.

You have to remember that this was more than fifty years ago, long before modern communication systems such as cell phones, the Internet and instant messaging. It's hard to understand now just how inconvenient it was when you needed to keep in touch. Back then it was phone calls and typewritten letters in the mail. E-mails weren't even in our dreams of things to come.

Donna dialed his number and handed me the receiver, which was of course on the end of a long, thick cord. "Hi, Chief. What's up?"

"Hi, Sam. I've been wondering if Miss Jones called you about working on the case. She asked me for your address. If she has, what did you find out?"

"She came to the office. And by the way, thanks for the great recommendation." I then related all the information to him about our visit to the hospital and talking to John Ashland. I also gave him the names of

28

the four men who were up for the movie roll, including John Ashland and the murdered actor Anthony Sparks.

He thanked me, saying he was looking forward to working with me again, and that he'd see me at my parents' wedding anniversary party next week. But he was curious about why they were having it on a Wednesday.

I related to him that Mom and Dad were leaving on Thursday and spending a few days in Turkey, before joining the cruise ship on Sunday morning for thirty days to celebrate their thirty-fifth wedding anniversary. And that they just wanted a few special friends to gather together to help them celebrate before they took off.

The Chief said he'd be there, and thanked me for the information again. He also said he'd let me know any information he might find out.

I hung up the phone and waited for Barcelona to call. An hour had passed but no call from her. I had other calls and each time my phone rang, I just about jumped out of my skin, hoping that it was her. Finally one hour and twenty-three minutes later her call came through.

"Hi, Sam. What time and where shall we meet?"

I gave no answer. I felt like my tongue was tied.

"Sam, Sam, are you there?"

"Uh yes … I'm just thinking. How about seven? I'll make reservations at the Rainbow Room if that's okay with you."

"Yes, it's one of my favorite places."

"Great. I'll pick you up at seven. Give me your address, Barcelona, so I can give it to the taxi driver."

She gave me her address. I couldn't believe that

she had said yes.

Oh, oh, I was thinking, *there goes my heart again!*

Chapter Nine

Just as soon as I hung up the phone I called my mom and dad. I'd not recognized Barcelona Jones when we first met, because I'd never really got involved in who's who in showbiz. But my mom and dad would know her for sure.

"Hello."

"Hi, Mom, this is Sam. How's everything going?"

"Just fine. How are you, Sammy?" That was mother's nickname for me. When I was younger I didn't like it, but now I find it comforting and loving.

"I'm great. Is Dad there?"

"He is. Do you want to talk to him?"

"Yes, but not just to him, but the both of you at the same time. Could he get on the other line?"

"Certainly. I hope everything is all right."

"Hi, Sam, what's up? Pray all is well with you."

"All is fine, Dad. I want you both to hear this together." I swallowed hard. Then continued, "I've found the girl I'm going to marry."

"Who is she, and where did you find her? Has she been lost?" That was Dad's sense of humor!

"Sammy, are you sure? And how come we haven't heard about her before? When did you meet her?"

I didn't want to answer Mom's question, but if I

didn't I knew she would persist. "Yesterday"

"What? You met her yesterday and you're already planning on marring her?" That was Mom's reply.

Then Dad cut in. "Okay, Sam, who is this woman who has apparently swept you off your feet? And does she feel the same way about you?"

"Not sure, Dad. Her name is Barcelona. She's one of my clients." I was afraid to tell them who she actually was, as I was sure that they'd both go into hysterics. I was beginning to wish that I hadn't called.

Mom spoke up next. Her voice quiet, and I detected much concern in it. I could tell she was worried that I'd be hurt, or maybe plunging into a not-so-good relationship. "Sammy, it's been such a short time. Have you gone out with her, or had any serious conversations about either of your future plans?"

"No, Mom, we haven't. I just know deep inside of me that she's the one I'm going to marry. We're going out to dinner tonight."

"Sammy, what does she do? You know you have a very good business, and as far as income you are pretty well set. Does she even have a job? And besides, you probably haven't even kissed her yet. And tell me again what did you say her name was?"

"Barcelona, Mom. Barcelona."

"Barcelona? There's a famous Broadway star with that name. Her last name is the same as ours. I'm sure that this Barcelona that you say you've fallen in love with is someone else."

Silence filled the air for a few seconds.

"Sammy, are you there?"

"Mom, Dad, the girl I'm going to marry *is* Barcelona Jones!"

That did it. They both went into hysterics – just as

I thought they would.

"Oh, Sammy, you're such a joker and I love you." That was Mom.

"That goes ditto for me, son. How do you come up with these crazy things?"

"No. Mom and Dad, I'm serious. I may bring her to your anniversary party on Wednesday, if that's okay with the two of you."

The phone went silent again. I could tell they were trying to hold back their laughter. I could hear muffled sounds coming from the receiver.

Dad finally spoke up. "Of course it's okay with us." Then after a long pause and hearing those muffled sounds again, he said, "Tell us again who you're going to marry."

"Barcelona Jones, the Broadway star."

That did it! This time I could hear them laughing out loud. They were no longer covering the mouthpiece of the phone. They were holding nothing back.

Chapter Ten

When I hung up the phone, my biggest regret was when I told them that I was bringing Barcelona to the anniversary party. I realized that if she didn't go, they would think for sure that I was playing a joke on them.

I finished some stuff around the office and told Donna to please close up whenever she was through. I wanted to go home, shower, put on my best outfit and pick up Barcelona for our date. At least that's what I was calling it. Barcelona was most likely going to call it a business dinner. Oh well, I was thinking whatever made her happy would definitely make me happy.

When I got out of the shower I heard my phone ringing. I ran to answer it, hoping it wasn't Barcelona calling to cancel our business-date-dinner.

"Hello, this is Sam."

"Sam, this is Chief Mead."

"Hi, Marty. This must be an official call."

"Yes, I'd like to confirm something with you. You did say that Peter Holmes was up for the male lead for the movie, *Murder on Broadway*? Right?"

"The Broadway actor. Yep, that's correct. Is he one of your suspects?"

"He *was* one of them, but not any longer."

"What cleared him? Does he have a foolproof alibi?"

"Yes, foolproof all right. He's in the hospital morgue."

"What happened? Another shooting?"

"No. This time it was poison."

"Poison? What kind, and when, and who found the body?"

"Don't know yet what kind. His body was found late this afternoon by his agent, Mike Larson. I'm wondering, can you come by the hospital and identify the body? I need another identification, as you know. I always like two or more."

"No, not me, I've never seen the guy before, but my date tonight can. If it's all right with her, I'll bring her by on our way to dinner."

"Okay, that will be great. Wait a minute, you have a date? This woman I have to see. I thought you were married to your job and didn't have time to date. That's what you told me a few months ago. Who is she? Is she someone I might know?"

"Maybe. I'll introduce her to you, if and when we get there."

I hung up and immediately dialed Barcelona. I was happy that when she gave me her address she also had written down her private phone number.

"Hello."

"Hi, Barcelona, this is Sam."

"Hi, Sam. Have you heard about Peter Holmes?"

"Yes, that's why I'm calling. News sure travels fast, doesn't it?"

"Yes, especially in show business. It was Mike Larson, his agent, who called me. He found the body."

"I know. And talking about the body, how do you

feel about identifying it? The Chief asked me, but of course I've never seen the guy. I told him I had a friend who knew him, and if she was willing I would bring her by. I didn't give him your name. Are you up to that?"

"Not really. I'm sure there are over a dozen cast and crew who could identify him. But if you think I should, then I will."

"Don't, if you're not comfortable with it. Please give me a couple of names of those who knew him, and I'll pass them on to the Chief."

Barcelona gave me three names with their telephone numbers. Then she said, "Thanks so much, Sam. You're a darling for understanding that I'm not comfortable with indentifying the body. And by the way, I'm looking forward to our date tonight."

Thump, Thump, Thump. My heart started to beat to the rhythm of a new love song.

Chapter Eleven

I called the Chief back and gave him the names Barcelona had given me. He said that would be fine, then added, "I'm disappointed that I won't get to meet your new girlfriend."

I asked him if they'd found out the kind of poison that killed Peter Holmes. He said there was still no news, so I told him I'd call him in the morning to see if they'd found out anything.

"Someday, Chief, someday – you are going to meet my new love, and are you ever going to be surprised!"

"Stop teasing me. Who is she?"

"Sorry, Marty, but I have to go. I'll call you tomorrow. Adios."

It was almost time to meet Barcelona. I left my building, hailed down a cab and gave the driver the address. When we arrived, Barcelona was waiting outside looking absolutely gorgeous. I jumped out of the taxi, held the door open and assisted her in.

I could tell she was still a little shaken by the death of Peter Holmes. Now two people she knew had been murdered. The first thing she asked me was, "Anything new on Peter Holmes' death?"

"No, nothing. I'll check with the Chief tomorrow and let you know just as soon as I find out anything, if it's all right with him."

It took us nearly fifteen minutes to arrive at the Rainbow Room, and most of those minutes I felt like my heart was going to jump right out of my mouth. We arrived right on time. When I made the reservations I'd asked for a quiet table by a window.

The restaurant was on the twenty-first floor. It was extremely popular at that time, and many famous people gathered there back then, but it's no longer in existence. It had a magnificent view of the city with all of the night lights shining off the many buildings in the distance. It was very beautiful and very romantic.

I had a tough time keeping my eyes off Barcelona, as did the many other dining room guests. She smiled at many of them as we were led to our table.

"Do you ever get used to everyone looking at you as you enter a room like this?"

"No, probably not, but I found out through the years that if I just look at them, smile and acknowledge them, they smile back, and then go back to their own conversations. After all, many of them have helped to make me what I am today, and I do so appreciate all of them."

"You are an amazing woman, Barcelona Jones."

She flashed that smile of hers, but it didn't hide the sweetness and also the embarrassment of all the attention she had created.

We had a great time. The dinner and service were excellent, just what one would expect at a place like the Rainbow Room. The conversation between the two of us was not only fun but very informative. We both laughed a lot and shared our growing up years.

She talked about her childhood, losing her parents at an early age and being raised by her grandmother whom she loved very much, and missed seeing while in New York. She also said she was looking forward to making the movie in Hollywood, as her grandmother lived in a suburb close by.

I told her about my folks and my sister Erica, and how we were all a very close family. Also about inheriting my father's detective agency and that soon he and my mother would be celebrating their thirty-fifth wedding anniversary. I wanted to invite her to the party, and I was waiting for the right moment.

I had a smile on my face thinking that my parents were probably still laughing about me dating Barcelona, and still thinking that it was a great big joke. I imagined them telling all their friends that I told them that I was bringing Barcelona Jones, the famous Broadway star to their party, and that I was going to marry her. And then breaking out into laughter with all their friends, telling them I was a big jokester.

My thoughts were interrupted when Barcelona asked, "What are you smiling at, Sam?"

"I was just thinking of my folks. When I told them I was having dinner with you tonight they didn't believe me. They thought I was pulling their leg. Do you mind if I call the photographer over to take our picture? That will really flabbergast them.'

"No, not at all. It sounds like fun."

"Thanks. My parents, believe it or not, are big fans of yours, just like my sister."

"And how about you, Sam?"

"I'm definitely becoming one of your biggest fans ever."

41

Chapter Twelve

When we left the Rainbow Room, the stars were out and it was a beautiful evening. I asked Barcelona if we could walk for a little while before we hailed a taxi. She agreed, so we walked in the direction of her apartment.

We stopped at many of the lighted windows of the stores along the way, and window-shopped.

I would jump in front of windows with their mannequins displaying the current fashions, and act like one of them. Barcelona would laugh so hard that sometimes tears rolled down her face. She told me later that was the night when she started to fall in love with me.

As the evening became more and more relaxed, I placed my hand in hers. She didn't pull back. I remember thinking that it was a very good sign. So feeling that this was the time, I decided to ask her if she would go with me to my parents' anniversary party.

"Barcelona, next Wednesday afternoon my parents are hosting a party before they leave for a month's cruise to celebrate their thirty-fifth wedding anniversary. Would you be available to join me for the occasion? I would be very pleased if you could. I'd like you to meet my family, and I know they'd love to meet you."

"I think it may be possible, Sam. I'd love to meet your mom and dad and the rest of your family. Let me check my schedule to make sure. I know I have an appointment with a friend in the morning, but I'm not sure about the rest of the day. I'll call you sometime tomorrow to confirm. Is that all right with you?"

"I'll be in and out of the office all day tomorrow. I plan on meeting with the Chief about the poisoning of Peter Holmes, plus I have some other investigating I must do. I would like to talk again with John Ashland and his agent Mike Larson. Besides, I'd like to see you before next Wednesday. How about Friday for breakfast or lunch? Then you can tell me if you're able to go with me."

"Lunch sounds good, Sam. What time?'

"How about twelve-thirty? There's a great place across from my office. It's small, but the food's great. It's reservations only, so if you can make it by then, I'll go ahead and call them."

"Twelve-thirty is fine for me. I'll meet you there. What's the name of the place?"

"It's called 'The Place to Eat.' You can't miss it."

We waved a taxi. As we got in, I was sorry that the evening was coming to an end. But all good things must end sometime. I looked over at Barcelona. She smiled and I reached over and took her hand. Again no resistance.

When we arrived at her apartment, there was an elevator but we both chose to walk the stairs instead, holding hands. I wanted to kiss her goodnight, but ...

There was a saying in those days that said, "Never kiss a girl on the first date. Wait for date two." But I was remembering what my mother said, about how did I know this was the girl I was going to marry because I hadn't even kissed her yet. My head was whirling. Should I or shouldn't I? I wanted to, just so I could tell my parents that I did, and she was still the girl I was going to marry.

Barcelona handed me the key. I opened the door and gave the key back to her. As she entered I held her hand a few seconds longer. I waited for the opportunity, but she went inside with the door still open, and said, "Goodnight, Sam."

Halfway down the stairs I turned around. She was still at the open door. She smiled, and I blew her a kiss.

My heart? You guessed it – thump, thump, thump!

Chapter Thirteen

Thursday

I woke up early the next morning, had my leisurely one cup of coffee and a piece of toast. This is something I did then, and still do, just about every day. When I opened up the morning paper that had been delivered to my door, the headlines were big and bold, and just as I anticipated: BARCELONA'S PLAY BECOMES A REALITY. *MURDER ON BROADWAY* IS JUST THAT, WITH A SECOND MURDER!

It retold the story of the murder and how the audience thought it was part of the play when they heard the screams and shouts behind the drawn curtain. It reminded the readers that actor Michael Sparks had really been shot, and that it wasn't until Barcelona came out between the curtains and asked if there was a doctor in the house, that the audience was convinced it was a real shooting.

It went on to report that Peter Holmes, another Broadway actor, had been found dead in his apartment. The paper suggested that the police should look for a connection between the two murders, since both of them had been reported to be up for the same lead in a Hollywood production of the play of the same name beginning next year.

The article went on to say that the cause of Mr. Holmes' death had not yet been released, but rumors said it was by a rare poison. It was either given to the deceased by someone or that he had ministered it to himself.

I waited until 9:10 and then called Marty – Chief Mead. He said there was still no news he could give me, and asked me to meet him around noon at the county morgue where the body of Peter Holmes had been transferred. He thought they would have the information for him by then, on what kind of poison had been used. I said I'd be there.

After I hung up, I went to the office. Donna was already there. I asked her to make two appointments for me sometime after two in the afternoon: one with John Ashland, who had now recovered from his peanut reaction, and the other with his agent, Mike Larson. I had Ashland's number but not his agent's. I asked Donna to call Ashland first, set up the appointment, and then ask him for Mike's phone number.

She asked me, "How far apart do you want the appointments, boss?"

"I'm not sure. Maybe make it with Ashland today and with Mike the agent tomorrow, if possible. If not, make them both tomorrow, about three hours apart."

I told Donna I wasn't sure how long it would take with Ashland, because I had no idea if he would want to talk.

"Ask them both if they can meet me here at the office."

I left for the County Morgue around 11:30 a.m. Donna still could not get through to Ashland when I left. She

48

had called about three times, getting no answer. Answering machines were only just coming onto the market back then, and it was no surprise that Ashland didn't have one. I told Donna to keep trying and I would check back with her around 1:00.

Chief Mead was already there when I arrived at the morgue. He informed me that there was no news yet, but that they were sure it was definitely a rare form of poison they hadn't come into contact with before. They mentioned that it was still possibly a suicide. The Chief said he wasn't buying it, and felt it was connected somehow to the death of Anthony Sparks.

The door opened and Dr. Edwards, the medical examiner, came over and said, "Well, we finally figured it out. Have either of you ever heard of the fugu fish?"

We both shook our heads.

"Its most common name is blowfish. Does that ring a bell?"

"Yeah," the Chief said. "Isn't that some kind of a poisonous Japanese fish?"

"Right, Chief. Actually it's a Japanese delicacy, but it must be properly filleted by a trained chef, because of its highly concentrated poison in its tissue. There have been reports of death to the Japanese people who try to prepare the fugu fish at home. Just a single drop of the poison can be fatal. It's more deadly than cyanide. There's no doubt in our minds that this is the poison that killed Michael Sparks.

I asked the doctor if he knew of any restaurants here that served that kind of fish. He said he'd never heard of any having blowfish on its menu.

I then turned to the Chief. "How about you, Chief?

Have you heard of any?"

"No, none that I know of. But remember this is New York City, and people can find just about anything they want for the right price."

The Chief and I thanked Dr. Edwards and we headed for the many fish markets on the ocean front harbor to snoop around and ask questions to anyone who was willing to talk.

We asked umpteen buyers but they all said, "No, we only sell fresh fish out of our waters."

Chapter Fourteen

I called Donna from the morgue, She said she had made an appointment with Ashland in my office at 3:00 p.m. I had about forty-five minutes to get there. I excused myself from the Chief, thanked him for his help, and promised to pass on anything useful I found out about the case. I neglected to tell him who my appointment was with. I was sure he'd want to be there, and I wanted to ask John Ashland questions with no interruptions. I felt that he would be more at ease if the Chief wasn't there.

I arrived at my office ten minutes before John Ashland. Donna mustered him in and I motioned for him to sit down. I was amazed how well he looked after his reaction to the peanut poisoning. He truly looked like a star, both in appearance and dress. When I saw him in the hospital he looked pale and drawn. I hadn't realized how close he must have come to death.

"Thanks for coming in, John, on such a short notice. You look really well. How are you feeling?"

"I'm feeling good now, but at times I feel a little worried. Barcelona has hinted that maybe the murder of Michael Sparks might have been meant for me.

That's why I'm here. If I can help in any way to solve this crime, I'm willing. I know I'll get a little concerned every time the first act ends with the shooting, thinking that the gun might have real bullets in it again. Believe me, I'm going to check that gun each night myself, just before the curtain goes up. Especially since Peter Holmes is now dead. Poisoning, so I hear. I keep wondering if I'll be the next victim."

He maintained eye contact as he continued. "I know I'm not here just for a visit, so please ask any questions you have. And let me know any information you find out. It may help me to be calm over all of this."

"Well, John ... is it all right if I call you by your first name?"

He nodded.

I continued. "As you know, I've been hired by Barcelona. She feels that the shooting was intended for you."

I neglected to say that for Barcelona my services were free. "So we want to find out as much as we can about how it could be possible for you to digest some kind of peanut extract into your body. Let's begin with Tuesday. What did you do from the moment you woke up until you were attacked by the severe reaction? Try not to leave anything out, no matter how small it may seem to you. Sometimes the most irrelevant thought helps us to solve a case. So think back and take your time. Close your eyes if you have to. It can help you to remember more."

"Let me see. I woke up at six, just like I do every morning, and had a sweet roll and two cups of coffee. I laid around, read the paper and then went over some of my lines for the evening performance. I kind of flubbed up on Monday night's performance in the second act. Then I went in and took my shower. When I got out, I heard the phone ringing. I ran in and answered it. It was Mike Larson, my agent. He wanted to meet me for lunch. He was actually returning the call I'd made to him the day before, when I'd left a message with his secretary to have him call me back.

"He said he wanted to talk to me about the new movie of the play, and that it was going to be a close race between all four of us for the lead. But since I was in the play, he thought I had a little edge in getting the part. He said that they were going to check with Barcelona, and he was wondering how my professional relationship with her was getting along. I told him fine."

I raised my eyebrows but said nothing. Better to let him talk, and listen carefully for any clues in what he said.

He shrugged. "Okay, I had some disagreements with Barcelona in the past, on another play. Anyway, I told Mike that all was now well. He said he needed to meet with me, so we arranged to meet at twelve-thirty at the Rainbow Room. They have great lunches and dinners, and we know many of the staff there and always run into someone we know. It's a fun place to go. After that, I was on my way home to rest before the evening performance. When I was close to my home I took very sick. Recognizing the symptoms, I took myself to the emergency room at St. Ann's hospital, and that's it."

"So you've been to the Rainbow Room many times. Do they know about your allergy?"

"Yes, they're all so helpful and always warn me if they think something that I order might affect my allergy. I usually try and order the same thing each time, although once in awhile I try something different. But that day I had my usual: cob salad, no dressing or nuts of course. I have to be careful. Sometimes they put nuts in dressing. I also had an ice coffee."

"Did anyone come over and talk to you? Maybe even leaned over your plate? Anything would help right now."

'Yes, a few came over to talk to me. Mostly congratulations on the success of the play. The ones who saw it said how much they enjoyed it. But no one to my knowledge leaned over my dish. I wouldn't have liked that at all."

"Did you leave the table for any length of time, maybe to go over to another table and talk to someone?"

"No, I'm not much of a table hopper."

"What was your conversation like, and why else did your agent want to talk to you? Was there another reason besides doing the movie?"

"He wanted to talk about my contract with him. He said he was going to fight for me to receive the part. And if I got it, he wanted a full ten percent. That's almost double the amount I pay him now."

"Did you agree?'

"I did. I knew that he represented the two actors who are now dead, but of course at that time I didn't know that they wouldn't be my competitors. So I said, 'Okay, if I get the part, I'll pay you the ten percent.' As far as I was concerned it would be worth it. A movie with Barcelona is a great push for my career."

He paused for a second, then said, "I remember now. I did get up and use the bathroom right after we placed our order, and when I returned our lunches were on the table."

"Okay, now we're getting somewhere. Did you taste anything different when you ate?"

"No, that's the problem. Very seldom can you taste anything different if peanut oil is mixed with all the spices and flavors. You can't possibly think that Mike Larson had anything to do with this, can you?"

"Anything is possible. By any chance, do you know who represents Charlie Long, the Hollywood actor who is also up for the part?"

"No, but I do know that Mike flew to Hollywood a couple of weeks ago. He said he was going there to check out Charlie Long, whatever that means."

Chapter Fifteen

I fiddled around the office for another hour or so, putting all the information in the order that Ashland had given me. It looked like Mike the agent, was our culprit. But it was much too early to be sure and to make an arrest. And besides, how and when would he have had an opportunity to put real bullets into the prop gun that killed Anthony Sparks?

Walking on the way home, my thoughts were no longer on the interview I had just completed, but were now on Barcelona and our lunch date. When I arrived home, the phone was ringing off its hook. It was Donna informing me that I had an appointment with Mike Larson, Ashland's agent, on Saturday at 1:00 p.m.

I lingered on it for a little while, wondering what would come out of our time together. Would I still think the agent was the guilty one, or would he shed some new insight on the two murders that would make me doubtful?

Eventually my thoughts returned to the person I was in love with, and wishing I was going to spend more time with her and not just a lunch break. It was early but I was tired, so I went to bed thinking of you-know-who.

Just when I was about ready to fall asleep, my telephone rang. I wasn't going to answer it, but then thought maybe the Chief had some news for me. I got out of bed and in a very grumpy voice said, "Hello, this is Sam."

"I'm sorry, Sam, is this a bad time to call you? You sound very irritated."

It was Barcelona.

"Sorry if I sounded ... distant. I had other things on my mind. This is a perfect time to call."

"I'm going to be free tomorrow morning as well as the afternoon, so I thought we could spend most of the day together. But I'll have to be back to the theater no later than six-thirty. Are you up for that?"

"Yes, and if I wasn't, I'd make free time for you. I was just thinking and hoping that we'd have more time together tomorrow. I'll pick you up in the morning at eight. Or is that too early for you?"

"No, that's okay. I'll set my alarm and be ready for you when you arrive. Will you be coming by taxi?"

"No, I'll bring my car so we can have breakfast out of the city. Have you ever been to the zoo?"

"No, but I've heard it's a great one."

"It's one of the best. I'll see you tomorrow morning at eight, in front of your building."

I was riding high. I was going to spend most of the day with the woman I was hoping that someday would not only be Barcelona Jones, but the new Mrs. Sam Jones.

Chapter Sixteen

Friday

I picked up Barcelona right on time, and we drove out of the city for breakfast at a place I'd stopped many times before, on the way to my folks' home. The breakfast was always good: eggs basted, bacon crisp but not burnt, and country fried potatoes that were the best I'd ever eaten. Plus your coffee cup was never empty.

I ordered the same for both of us. I knew I couldn't go wrong.

During our meal I brought up the interview I'd had with John Ashland, now that he was out of hospital. I wanted to get it out of the way so the rest of the day we could zero in on other things: like where is our relationship going? Or, can I see you again? And again? Just thinking about it made me a little nervous.

I asked Barcelona, "John Ashland said that at one time you two had a disagreement. What was that all about?"

"It was over a part in one of the plays we were doing together. I'd already worked with John a couple of plays back. He wasn't very nice to some of the cast players, but was okay toward me though. When I did my next play there were two who were up for the male lead, and John was one of them.

"The director, producers and I had a meeting. I suggested we use the other actor. John heard about it and got very angry, saying some terrible things to me. A few days later he called and said he was sorry and would I forgive him. Of course I said yes.

"During the next couple of years we ran into each other many times. He was always sweet and apologetic. When this play we're doing now came up, and his name was mentioned, I agreed he'd be great for the part.

"I also agreed he'd be great for the movie. My contract says I can meet with the producers and help choose who will be the male lead to play Billy the bully. We narrowed it down to John Ashland and Charlie Long. But so far no decision has been made."

"Are you leaning to anyone special who you'd like to work with, and feel would be the best Billy?"

"They both would be great, but I'm thinking of Charlie Long. The times I've met him he appears very nice, and is someone I could like to work with either in this picture or one in the future – if there is another one. Everyone I've talked to says Charlie is great to work with and always congenial. I'd like working with someone like that, especially making my first movie. I think John would be a little more difficult and demanding. Charlie is flying out here and we'll be meeting and reading together for the director. I'm hoping to get to know him better."

I must have had a concerned look on my face, for Barcelona said, "Don't worry, Sam. He's bringing his wife. Would you like to meet him?"

I assured her I would. She said that she'd make the arrangements and that maybe the four of us could meet for lunch or dinner. They would be here on Tuesday to review the play, and that maybe we could all meet on Wednesday afternoon.

I mentioned about the poison that had killed Michael Sparks, and that it was from a highly poisonous fish called fugu. She said she'd never heard of such a fish.

As we left the restaurant, I said, "Let's not talk about the case any longer. Let's just enjoy the rest of the day."

Barcelona agreed, and I told her a little about the zoo that had many types of animals, and that the grounds were very beautiful. I said that it was huge, and we could spend all day there and still not see everything.

"Good, I love animals of all types. And I hope they have popcorn and corn dogs. I love them. In a few hours I know I'll be hungry again. They do have them, don't they?"

"I think so. I'm not sure, but if that's what you want for lunch, I'll do my best to find them for you."

When we arrived, there was a waiting line to enter the gates. It was a great day and there was no need for even a light sweater. The day was perfect. Just what I was hoping for.

Barcelona was like a little kid enjoying every moment, and of course I kept falling more and more in love with her.

As we looked in every cage of each animal I would play like I was one of them, just as I'd done when we looked into the store windows while walking on our first date. That night, I had mimicked being a mannequin in the windows!

This was much more fun. When we saw the monkeys I acted like one of them, throwing my arms in the air and walking like them. When we looked at the bears I pounded my chest like I was Tarzan. When we gazed at the lions I roared and prowled around. Coming to the giraffes I stretched my neck as far as I could, moving it back and forth while strutting like I was one of them.

I didn't care who was watching me or what the other people were thinking and, as far as I could tell, neither did Barcelona.

She laughed, held her stomach and wiped the tears from her eyes. And as I looked into those eyes I could see something else in them besides the tears of joy falling down from her cheeks. There were moments when the looks she gave me and the smile on her face were revealing to me that she was also falling in love.

Chapter Seventeen

We walked across one of the three bridges in the park-like setting in the zoo grounds. Each bridge crossed over a small man-made lake, known by many as the zoo with the three bridges. When we arrived in the middle of one of the bridges we stopped. Both of us leaned over and rested our hands on the railing. I bravely moved my hand until it touched hers.

In silence, we watched as a mother duck led her four babies to the other side of the lake. As if on cue we both stood up and faced each other ... this was the time. I leaned my head down, almost touching her lips. I waited, she moved toward me and our lips met. I can't say I saw fireworks, but I heard the sounds as they were exploding in my head.

We broke away. I kissed her lips again but this time very gently. I told her that I loved her. She responded with the words I wanted to hear. "I love you too, Sam."

Just then we heard from the other side of the bridge, "Peanuts, popcorn. Come and get your peanuts and popcorn."

Barcelona took my hand and we both ran to the vendor, laughing all the way. I felt like a little boy excited about what was happening.

After we got our popcorn we saw a bench under a huge shade tree. I led Barcelona to it, both of us with our popcorn bags in hand. As we settled down on the bench, Barcelona said, "In my wildest dreams I never thought anyone could fall in love with someone on a second date. Especially me."

"It's possible," I said. "After all, I fell in love with you *before* our first date."

We leaned forward to each other as our lips met again. We didn't care that our popcorn bags had slid off of our laps and spilled all over the ground.

All I could think of was my heart and the sound that was coming from it!

Chapter Eighteen

On the drive home, I asked Barcelona, "You never told me how you got your name. Is it for real, or is it a stage name? I understand many stars give themselves a new name, or their agents do."

"Sam, Barcelona is my honest to goodness real name."

"How did you get it? I remember you said that your parents had their reasons."

"Good memory, Sam. It was their second wedding anniversary. They were in Barcelona, Spain celebrating. Many of my school mates used to ask me the same question. One day I asked my parents about it. They looked at each other, smiled, and my mom said, 'We were wondering when you would ask us that.'

"My father cleared his voice, and said, 'Well, you got your name because you were conceived in Barcelona.'

"Up to then, my name to me was just a name. Now I was embarrassed each time somebody asked me about it. So I began telling everyone that it was my great grandmother's name who was born in Barcelona, Spain. Then one of my so-called friends sold the story of my real name to *Photoplay*

Magazine. Since then, I'm not asked about it very often anymore. But now I must confess my friends get a laugh out of it when somebody does ask. They wait to see my reaction and hear what I tell them."

"Great story, my love. I was born in Chattanooga, Tennessee, so I must say I'm happy my folks didn't name me Chattanooga!"

"Sam, you're so funny. That's one of the many reasons I fell in love with you."

We arrived at the theater a little early, which Barcelona was very pleased about. I walked her to the back stage door where I leaned over to kiss her. She put her hands on my chest to restrain me.

"Sam, there are things we must talk about. Even though I've confessed to you that I love you, my career is still very important to me. I want to make sure you're not going to ask me to give it up."

"I'd never do that, just as I don't expect you to ask me to give up being a private detective because you may think it's dangerous. Your career is you. I'm in love with you. Why would I ask you to change?"

"Thanks, Sam. That means a lot to me. And don't worry, I'd never ask you to give up *your* work."

"When will I see you again, Barcelona? Soon will not be soon enough!"

"Tomorrow and Sunday are out for me. We have a matinee and an evening performance on both of those days each week. Monday I'll be meeting with the producers and the director. Charlie Long will be there from Hollywood to discuss the movie roll. I'm not sure about Tuesday. They may want me to meet again with all of them. I also would like to spend some time getting acquainted with Charlie."

I put my head down, looking worried about the part of Barcelona spending time with Charlie Long. She looked at me and patted my head. It was more like how one would pat a little dog.

"Remember, Sam, he's married, and his wife's coming with him. We'll all be meeting for lunch or dinner soon after they arrive."

I nodded my head, put my tongue out, panted and wiggled my backside like a happy little puppy.

I gave Barcelona a kiss on the forehead and then a quick kiss on the lips. I said my goodbyes and told her I'd be looking forward to Tuesday.

I turned and wiggled my way to my car, only turning around when I reached it. She was waving and shaking her head. I watched until she entered the building and closed the stage door.

Chapter Nineteen

I had almost forgotten that I had an appointment the next day myself. This one was with Mike Larson, the agent. I was also hoping I'd be able to spend some time with Charlie Long alone, as I had a few questions I wanted to ask him too. I was thinking that maybe Tuesday would bring me the opportunity.

I stopped off at the first florist I saw and ordered a dozen white roses. I remembered that somewhere in our conversation over the last two dates Barcelona had said that she loved white roses. I also ordered one red rose to be arranged in the middle of the dozen white ones. I wrote on a card, *THE RED ROSE REPRESENTS MY HEART THAT I HAVE GIVEN TO YOU . . . SAM*. I gave the florist the address and told them to deliver the roses in the morning.

I have continued to send Barcelona this floral arrangement on special dates that mean a lot to the two of us. After we were married and on the twelfth of each month, I give her a heart gift of some kind. The twelfth is the date of our wedding day. I guess I'm just a romantic.

Saturday morning I got up and had my coffee and a piece of toast. I went to the office and called the Chief.

He said he also had talked with John Ashland. We compared our notes and couldn't find anything different. The Chief had even checked with Ashland's doctor and confirmed that the actor did indeed have a serious reaction to peanuts. Besides, John Ashland wasn't our suspect. We were both leaning on the agent, Mike Larson. I was looking forward to our interview and hoping that after it was through, the case would be closer to being solved.

I took care of some paperwork and received two phone calls. One was a return call from a new client who was looking for a lost brother whom the caller thought might have been murdered. The other was from Charlie Long in Hollywood.

I said that I knew of him, and he told me that he had received two threatening notes on his life. He said he hadn't told anyone about the notes, not even his wife. He also said he'd be in New York on Monday, and since I was highly recommended by a friend, he was wondering if I could meet with him.

We set up a time on Tuesday evening. I told him I was sorry but I had to end our conversation as I had a client in my outer office waiting to see me. Before we hung up, I did ask him where the threatening notes were mailed from. He said from one of the post offices in the L.A. area.

I looked up in surprise when Donna escorted Mike Larson into my office. I had thought of him being older and a little overweight. Don't ask me why, because I don't know. Just a mental picture from what I'd heard about him. I often do this when I speak with someone on the phone, but I'm usually wrong after I meet them. And I was wrong again.

Mike Larson was in his early thirties, and as the

saying goes, fit as a fiddle. He was dressed smartly and expensively right down to his shoes. But what amazed me the most about Mike the agent was that he was very personable. I liked him right away. I had to remind myself that he was one of our prime suspects for the murders of Peter Holmes, Anthony Sparks and the attempted murder of John Ashland.

Chapter Twenty

Mike Larson said yes to the coffee I offered him, which most people don't. In fact, I remember he poured his own coffee, picked up his cup and walked over and sat in one of the chairs facing my desk. I watched him as he did all this with so much confidence. I was wondering if he was putting on an act for me, or if this was really his personality. I also wondered if he knew he was our prime suspect in the case. He gave no indication of either.

My first question to him was why did he fly to Hollywood to talk to the actor Charlie Long? While I was watching him, the thought came to me that he could have mailed the threatening notes to the actor while he was there.

His answer was calm, and with much confidence he said, "Not sure how you knew about that, but I had heard that Charlie was looking for a new agent. His agent had retired and he wasn't happy with the one who was taking his place. So I flew out there to see if I could sign him up. Charlie's very hot right now, and I wanted to pitch myself to him.

"Besides, when I called him to make the appointment he was very impressed that both John

Ashland and Peter Holmes were my clients. I'd set up the appointment some days before Peter was murdered, and before the attempt on John's life. "

"How long were you in the L.A. area?"

"Three nights and four days. I met with Charlie twice while I was there. I'm known in this business as a go-getter. Charlie's a really nice guy and not affected by his overnight stardom. Both times we met, his wife was also there. She didn't say much, but you got the feeling that she would have a big influence on his decision. She's beautiful enough to be a movie star herself, and also, by the way, just as nice as he is. They make a very handsome couple."

I was wondering if he knew that Barcelona and I were a couple, and also if he would have given us the same compliment. Probably not. Barcelona of course is very beautiful, but me, that's another story.

"Tell me, Mike … if I may call you that." He nodded, so I continued. "How long have you known John Ashland, and what happened when the two of you had lunch together the day he was poisoned?"

"I've known John for about seven years. He was an up-and-coming actor and wanted to change agents. At the time, I was just starting out as an agent and looking for clients. A friend introduced us and we hit it off okay, so I signed him up for a ridiculously low percent. I saw great potential in him, which is why I agreed on a low percent of his earnings.

"Our lunch meeting was to inform him that if I sold him to the producers and director for the movie roll for *Murder on Broadway*, I would raise my take to ten percent. I had a contract with me for him to sign if he was agreeable. He knew that I was also representing Peter Holmes and had met with the head honchos for the movie on his behalf."

He went on to say that John Ashland agreed and signed the contract, and that the rest of their lunch meeting was frivolous although a little cold in conversation. He said that he didn't think Ashland was happy about the contract, but he didn't want to look for a new agent at this late time of negotiations. He felt he had a pretty good chance of being given the part, and didn't want to make any waves.

"Mike, John Ashland said that some other people came to your table and talked to him, mostly about the death of Peter Holmes. Did you notice anyone close enough to his meal who might have been able to slip some kind of peanut extract onto his dish of food? You do know he's allergic to all kinds of peanut stuff, right?"

"Of course I do. Anyone who's ever worked with him or is a friend of John's knows of his allergy. There was no one whom I saw standing that close to him who could have put anything on his plate."

"Did either you or John leave the table for any length of time?"

"Yes, I saw a new client at another table and went over to say hello, and to tell him I was negotiating for a part for him in a movie. It wasn't the lead but a minor part. But it was a speaking part. He was very excited. When I returned to the table, John excused himself saying he was going to the restroom. That's about all that happened that I can remember."

"And that's about all *I* have, Mike. Thanks for coming in. And if you think of anything that might help the case, please give me a call."

I got up, shook Mike Larson's hand and walked him to the outer door. As likeable as he was, he was still our number one suspect – and I'm not too often wrong.

Chapter Twenty-One

I called Chief Inspector Marty Mead and asked him if he had any news for me. He said, "Nothing substantial. How about you?"

I told him about my talk with Mike Larson, and we both agreed that the agent would have had an opportunity to put something in John Ashland's food while he went to the restroom. The Chief said he was going to look into Mike Larson's character a little more to see what he could find out about him. I asked him how he would do that, and he said he'd check with his neighbors, his school and friends, and that he would definitely keep me informed. I was going to volunteer my expertise, but didn't feel it was needed. The Chief would be doing exactly what I would have done.

As I left the office I walked past the Shuster Theater but this time I looked up at the marquee and saw the name of the one I was in love with – in big bold letters. I was still in amazement thinking how was it possible that the name I was saying out loud was the woman I knew I was going to marry. I decided to go home and clean up, and then return to the theater and become a stage-door Johnny. That was what they used to call the guys who waited after each performance for the stars to come out the back door of the theater, and ask for a date. I was hoping that Barcelona would be completely surprised and happy to see me.

I stopped off at one of the flower vendors and bought a single long stemmed red rose, and waited for Barcelona to come out the back door. The door opened and there she was, looking very beautiful. She was ready to greet her fans and the press who were waiting for her with me.

I stood in the back shadows. After she had smiled, signed autographs and thanked everyone, I came out holding my one red rose. She saw me and her smile grew larger, but I could tell she wasn't ready for the world to know just yet that we were a twosome, especially with the press being there.

So I winked at her, smiled and moved my head in the direction around the building in an alley. Then I waited patiently for her to meet me there. What seemed like hours were only minutes. She came around the alley smiling. I embraced her, kissed her on the forehead and then on the lips. Her response was overwhelming.

We broke away, and I said, "I love you, Barcelona Jones. I've waited for someone just like you for a long time. Now that I have found you, I'll never let you go."

I kissed her again, softly at first, then more passionately. She pulled away. "Sam, please remember where we are."

I looked around. The alley was empty. I looked at her and we both began to laugh. I said, "I know it's so full of people, but I can't control myself. I feel like the two of us are the only ones here."

"Oh, Sam, you're so funny. Remember, I can't stay

up too late. I have two more performances tomorrow. But I'm glad you came here tonight."

"How about a quick snack? I promise I'll get you home early."

"If you promise." She looked at the red rose I'd given her. "And thanks, Sam, for giving me your heart."

Chapter Twenty-Two

I took Barcelona home early just as I'd promised, kissed her softly on the lips and told her goodnight. I had asked the cab driver to wait, because I knew I wouldn't linger at her door and keep her up any later.

I went straight home and went to bed. I couldn't fall asleep, as my thoughts were not only on Barcelona, but on my parents. I could hardly wait to see their faces when I introduced them to her. I was unable to wipe the smirk off of my face as I lay there in bed.

The next morning was Sunday, and I decided to go out for breakfast and then to church. I wasn't a churchgoer at that time, even though my parents did raise Erica and me in church, along with Sunday school and camps. The whole works! I still believed in God, but church just wasn't my thing any longer. As for Erica, she and her husband Rick and the kids were very involved in their church and had asked me many times to go with them. I always said I would, someday when I could find time, which I never did.

There was a little church just a couple of blocks away from my home that I had passed by many times. When I woke up that morning I thought about a walk in the park, thanking God for putting Barcelona in my life, but church sounded like a better idea. When I reached the church, the sign in the front said TODAY'S SERMON WILL BE *BEING THANKFUL*. Wow ... just what I was looking for. So I went in.

There were about one hundred people there, all friendly and very welcoming. The sermon was good, about being thankful for the blessings we'd received. Then the Pastor encouraged us to take a few moments to thank God for something or someone that was a special blessing to us.

I knew I was in the right place, but wasn't sure if it was God who led me there, or just a coincidence. Of course, my thankfulness that morning was to God for sending Barcelona to me.

Chapter Twenty-Three

Tuesday
Our lunch date for me to meet with Barcelona and Charlie Long and his wife had been changed to Tuesday. I could hardly wait for the time I would be spending with Barcelona, even if Charlie Long the actor and his wife would be there.

I was trying to figure out a way to tell Charlie that I hadn't told anyone about our conversation on the phone, when my phone rang. It was Barcelona confirming the time for our lunch date. She said when she told Charlie that a friend named Sam Jones was going to join them, he'd looked a little perplexed and she was wondering if I knew why. I didn't want to lie to her so I told her I had an appointment with him that evening about the case.

I added, "After all, he's one of the men up for the male lead and I wanted to ask him a few questions." I assured Barcelona I hadn't mentioned we were going to have lunch together, since it wasn't a sure thing. I asked her to be discreet about the matter, because Charlie Long hadn't mentioned our appointment to his wife as he didn't want to worry her.

"That's okay, Sam. I don't want to pry into your affairs about work. I was just curious about why

Charlie looked so strange when I mentioned your name. I'll see you this afternoon at the Rainbow Room at one-thirty. Our reservations have already been made."

I took a deep breath to steady myself. "I can hardly wait to see you. I've been waiting for this lunch date for months."

Barcelona gave a little laugh. "Oh, Sam, I wonder how many times I'm going to be telling you how funny you are through our very long-lasting relationship."

"Thousands and thousands of times, I hope. I'll never get tired of it."

"Goodbye, Sam. I have a feeling you're just trying to keep me on the line. See you soon."

"Uh, uh..."

"Goodbye, Sam."

We hung up and I started to count the minutes away until 1:30 came. I got to the Rainbow Room early and waited patiently for the three of them. Charlie and his wife arrived about ten minutes after I did. The only reason I recognized them was because of what Mike Larson said: that they were truly a handsome couple.

I walked over quickly and introduced myself, without letting anyone know that Charlie and I had talked on the telephone. In about three minutes Barcelona arrived. She saw us talking and knew that there was no need for any introductions.

I wasn't sure if I should shake her hand or give her a hug and a kiss. She walked up to me and kissed me on the cheek. I started to laugh but controlled myself with just a smile. I hugged her in return, missing her lips and also kissing her on the cheek. A beautiful smile came over her face. At that moment that was enough for me.

She walked over and talked to the maitre d' who of course knew who she was. He then escorted us to our table.

We had a very nice time and the four of us agreed that we had found new friends. I could tell that Barcelona was leaning very heavy on Charlie Long being her co-star, by the way the conversation was going.

Sometime during our table talk, Charlie's wife asked us if we were a couple. I remember saying, "Is it that obvious?"

She replied, "Obvious to me. How long has this being going on? You both act like you've known each other for years."

Barcelona and I looked at each other and she said, grinning, "Not too long. About seven days."

"Wow," Charlie said with a smile. "It must have been love at first sight."

"For me, yes. It took Barcelona a little more time. About five days."

We all agreed we'd like to meet again, but living so far apart we weren't sure when or how. We promised if we ever got to Hollywood, or they came back to New York, we would definitely make it a foursome again.

Charlie said he had an appointment, while his wife went New York shopping. Barcelona said she had many errands before she had to return to the theater. All three of them then looked at me.

"Me? I have to go to the office. There are things I must do. Besides, I also have an appointment."

I tried not to look at Charlie Long, as I wanted no recognition that he was my appointment. I gave Barcelona a hug and told her I was looking forward to

tomorrow and spending most of the day with her.
   She hugged me back, saying, "Me too."

Chapter Twenty-Four

When I arrived at my office, Donna said, "A Mr. Long has just called. He said his wife was going shopping earlier than he expected, and he wanted to know if he could come earlier. He said he'll be here at five, unless he hears back from you."

I remember telling Donna to please call Charlie back and tell him that would be fine. Then I asked her if she would please leave around 4:30. There was no need to explain. She understood, as this type of thing had happened many times before. There never was any question; she just honored my requests. It wasn't because I didn't trust her, but I knew that the client would feel more comfortable not having her here, especially if it was someone famous, as in this case.

When Charlie arrived I got up from my desk and shook his hand. We had some small talk about our time together at lunch. He was no longer just a name, he had now become a friend. Yes, another one of those short-time things.

Charlie got right to the point and handed me the two threatening notes. They both said the same thing, and looked like they both had been typed on the same typewriter. I read the note out loud. "If you want to be where Michael Sparks is, go ahead and accept the movie part."

Charlie then said a little nervously, "And we both know where Michael is. … In the city morgue." He paused for a moment and then continued. "I talked to some other famous actors at the studio about threatening notes, without telling them about mine. Some said that they've received them, but nothing has ever happened. But because of Michael Sparks' and Peter Holmes' deaths, and the attempt on John Ashland's life, I *am* a little concerned."

"Yes, and you have a right to be. Tell me about your time with Mike Larson, the agent."

"Not much to tell. I met with him twice while he was in Hollywood."

I interrupted and asked if it was before or after he had received the two notes. He said before.

I asked, "Did he call you, or did you call him?"

"He called me. He said he'd heard that I wasn't happy with the guy who bought out my former agent's business. He wanted to fly out to Hollywood and talk with me about signing up with him. I asked him what other clients he had, and he read off a list. I was impressed, so said, 'Sure. Come on out and we'll talk.'

"We set up a time. I liked him and told him that my contract was up in about three months, and that I'd sign with him. I asked Mike to send me a contract and I'd look it over."

"Has he sent you one? And if he did, is it honorable, and did you sign it?"

"No. That's the funny part. Mike never did send it to me. He didn't seem like a guy who would forget or not get on it right away. It's been about two weeks. He seemed to me to be a go-getter who wouldn't forget things like that."

I agreed. I told him that I'd met Mike Larson and also liked him right away, and that he seemed like a guy who would send the contract out as soon as he got back to New York. That puzzled both of us.

I told Charlie I would investigate the two threatening notes, and that I had some contacts in the L.A. area. I knew they could help me investigate them. I told him not to worry, but to be careful, and if another note popped up to give me a call. We said our goodbyes as I walked him to the door of the outer office. I went back to my desk to try and sort things out.

That's when the thought came to me that the only possible reason I could think of why Mike Larson didn't send Charlie Long the contract, was because he knew he wouldn't be alive to fulfill it.

Chapter Twenty-Five

Wednesday

I picked Barcelona up at 9:30 the next morning as planned. The drive to my folks' home was a little over one and a half hours. I wanted to stop for breakfast at the same little restaurant we did the day we went to the zoo. And I wanted to show Barcelona the area I was raised in, before we arrived at my mom and dad's party. My folks had bought their present home, over thirty years before, and as the saying goes, for a song. I knew Barcelona would love it.

I hadn't told her anything about the home. I wanted it to be a surprise, because eventually when my parents either sold it, or my sister and I inherited it, I would buy it or buy Erica out. We had both agreed on this, as Erica and her husband had already bought their dream home. So I was hoping that Barcelona would love it as much as I did, so we could raise our children there.

We stopped for breakfast and soon it was to become Barcelona's favorite place for breakfast. That's where we always stopped to eat whenever we went to visit my mom and dad. We continued this even after the kids came. It was one of our many family outings.

When we arrived in our little town I took Barcelona to the school I attended; to the football field where I broke my leg; the only movie house where I saw all my favorite movies; the two gas stations; and the one and only super market.

The town hadn't changed much since I was a kid. At that time we had maybe 4,000 people. The new sign read 10,200 AND STILL GROWING. I explained to Barcelona that it couldn't grow much more as there wasn't much land for new houses, which was why most of the homes had gone sky high in value. Every once in a while she said, "I could live here. It's so quaint, and the homes are beautiful and well maintained. I like your little town."

We walked through the only city park, held hands and sat on my favorite bench. I told her it was on that bench where I got my first kiss from Sally.

Barcelona wanted to know who Sally was. I told her she would meet her that afternoon at the party.

"Should I be jealous, Sam?"

"No way. She's always remained a good friend, not only to me but my whole family. Besides, she's happily married and has four kids. They, along with Erica's two, all call me Uncle Sam."

Time was moving quickly and it was now time to go the party. I asked Barcelona if she was nervous. She said she was, a little, but because of what I'd told her about my parents she was excited to meet them. I couldn't wait to see the looks on their faces when I introduced them to her.

The homes on Park Lane were all beautiful, even though most of them were over forty years old. The owners took pride in their investments. The lawns and driveways were spick and span. Each home was set back from the street and had a long driveway with many trees and green lawns. It was very impressive. Barcelona was taking it all in, and I could tell she too was impressed. I turned into the driveway of my folks' home. There was a sign that read JONES DRIVE. The drive was long and circular. I held my breath waiting, to hear what Barcelona would say. At first no comments, then just what I was hoping for.

"Sam, this is lovely. And look at the home. It's magnificent. I could spend the rest of my life in a home just like this. How fortunate you were to be raised in a town like this and in this beautiful home. From what you've told me of your parents, you've been blessed."

Cars were already parked on the side of the driveway. I parked where it would be hard to see inside the car. I asked Barcelona to remain in the car for just a few minutes.

"Why, Sam? What are you planning?"

"Just my surprise for Dad and Mom. I'll be right back."

I got out of the car and walked to the front entrance and rang the door bell. Both Mom and Dad answered.

Mom said, "Sammy, why didn't you just come in? You know an occasion like this the door is always open."

Then they both looked around and then at each other, shrugged their shoulders with a mischievous grin on their faces, letting me know that it was just me, and no Barcelona Jones.

Dad said, "I see you're all alone. Where is this Miss Jones woman?"

Mom patted him on the chest. "Never you mind. She's probably hiding in the bushes somewhere."

They both snickered and chuckled at the same time.

"Oh, Sammy, you're such a joker, but we love you even if you are alone. Come on in and join the party. There are other pretty, single girls here."

"You two go inside. I left something in the car. I'll be right in."

I went back and got Barcelona, giving my parents time to join their guests. Then Barcelona and I walked into the enormous living room where all the guests were chatting and having a great time.

I stood on the landing of the entrance, cleared my throat loudly, and when the talking stopped and everyone was looking at us, I said, "Family and friends, may I introduce to you Miss Barcelona Jones."

Of course, Mom and Dad recognized Barcelona immediately, as I knew they would. There were clapping of hands and my mother and father came rushing over with big smiles on their faces. With too much pride in my voice, I said, "Mom, Dad, this is Barcelona."

My mom gave her a big hug and I heard her whisper in her ear, "I don't know how he got you here, but make him pay for it with his life."

Dad hugged her, and said, "Welcome to our home, Barcelona. What did he bribe you with to get you here?"

I turned to Barcelona, I could see she was enjoying every minute of it. As they walked away, I said, "They still think it's a joke. This is going to be a fun party."

94

To myself I was thinking that it was no joke, and that soon I was going to marry Barcelona Jones. It was still hard for me to believe.

Chapter Twenty-Six

After the party my mom and dad, Erica, Rick and the kids, and Barcelona and I stayed around and chatted for about an hour. The party was fun and everyone seemed to have had a nice time wishing my folks a happy thirty-fifth wedding anniversary and a great voyage.

We talked on many subjects, and of course they asked Barcelona a lot of questions about the theater. No one seemed brave or direct enough to ask if our relationship was serious. They liked her so much that I was thinking they were probably afraid that we'd say that we were just friends, and they were hoping for something more.

As we left, my folks told Barcelona that she was welcome to come back any time, with or without me. All four of them looked at me with a pleading look that said they wanted more information about our relationship. I shrugged my shoulders and made a sad face. They looked so disappointed, and I was trying not to laugh as I was enjoying every second of it immensely.

On the way home I asked Barcelona where she thought our relationship might be going, and if she thought we could have a future together: with her being a big star on Broadway, and soon to be in the movies, and me a private detective.

She was silent for a moment, then said, "Yes of course, Sam, I feel the two of us may have a grand future together."

I wasn't sure of the "MAY" word, so I pulled the car over under a street light because I wanted to see the reaction on her face when I presented the next question.

"Barcelona, if I gave you an engagement ring, would you accept it?"

I think it took her a little by surprise, for she said, "Sam, are you asking me to marry you? I've heard of many ways that men have proposed to my friends. Basically they're all the same. If this is a proposal, I have never heard of one quite like it. But knowing you and your funny personality, I want to make sure. So, Sam, are you asking me to marry you and to become your wife?"

"Yes, my love, that's exactly what I'm doing.... Barcelona Jones, will you marry me and become my wife?"

"In that case, Sam, I would love to be your wife. Yes I will marry you, and yes I will accept an engagement ring. And, Sam, I love you and your last name ... Jones."

With that, I leaned over and gave her my most passionate kiss. As we pulled away she said, "Remember, Sam, the engagement ring isn't a marriage license, so it doesn't give us the freedom to sleep together. I want to wait for our wedding night. I want that moment to be special. So please, Sam, don't pressure me."

"I would never pressure you, my love, into doing

anything you don't want to do, no matter what it may be. I love you and I want always to be there for you. If you want to wait for our wedding night, then that's exactly what I also want to do."

I remember then leaning over and kissing her on the forehead and then on the lips.

"Thank you, Sam. Another reason why I've fallen in love with you. I know you'll always think of me first in any situation that may come up in our future lives together."

Barcelona told me her ring size and I noted it down. I wanted everything to be perfect. When I got into my car I put it in drive and felt like I was driving on the streets of gold in the Heavenly Kingdom.

Chapter Twenty-Seven

When we arrived at the apartment where Barcelona was staying, she said that the next day she was having a fitting on one of the dresses for the play. It was for 11:30 in the morning and it would take about an hour. And after the fitting she wanted to come to my office and bring lunch for us and Donna. She was hoping to get to know Donna better.

I thought it was a great idea and Barcelona made me promise not to tell anyone about our plan to become engaged until after she and her agent informed the press. Of course it was all right to tell my family, but no one else.

"I'll hold my tongue." While saying that, I held my tongue with my thumb and forefinger, repeating what I had just said. The words came out all mumbled and jumbled.

"Sam, I'm serious."

"I know you are, so don't worry. No one will say anything until after you've informed your fans through the magazines, the papers, and I'm sure the radio and TV.

"Thanks, Sam. I'll see you tomorrow around one o'clock, if not sooner."

I gave her a goodnight kiss and made sure she was

safely inside her apartment before driving home to call my dad.

I knew he had a friend in the jewelry business, and I'd already started to think up a design for an engagement ring on the way to my place. He gave me the address and I thanked him, giving him no other information.

"Why do you want his number? Is this another joke of yours? I know you love playing pranks on your old parents."

"You'll find out soon enough – like after you return from your ... how many honeymoons does this make?"

I knew that he'd tell Mom, and both of them would be so curious that they'd be up half the night trying to guess what this was all about. They'd be wondering if this was real or another game I was playing. Now I was the one doing the laughing. I must confess again that I was truly enjoying myself.

Chapter Twenty-Eight

Thursday

I got up early the next morning, and had my usual breakfast. When I was through, I made an appointment with the Chief for late afternoon at his office. We decided to go over both of our notes together carefully, to see if we could come up with something substantial.

After the call was finished I got dressed and headed for the office. When Donna came in I told her about Barcelona bringing us lunch about 1:00. She gave me another of her looks. This one said, "What's going on?" but she said nothing.

By 1:00, Barcelona hadn't arrived. By 2:00 I was getting worried, and at 2:30 the phone rang. It was her.

"Hello ... Sam?"

I could tell by her voice that something was wrong.

"Barcelona, are you crying?"

"I'm in the hospital. I was almost killed on the way to your office."

"Killed? What hospital are you in? I'm coming right over."

"St. Ann's."

"Don't say another word. I'm on my way."

I arrived at the hospital in breaking time, found out Barcelona's room number, and ran to it as quickly as I could. She was in bed. When she saw me, the tears freely spilled out. I put my arms around her as she shuddered and shook with fear. Her left arm and shoulder were black and blue.

"Barcelona, what happened? Do you feel like talking about it? If you're not comfortable talking about it just yet, that's fine. I'm staying right here."

She took a deep breath, and it obviously caused her pain as she did it. "I was going to cross the street to go to your office. The signal was red, so I waited for the green light. I don't know exactly how it happened, but I fell in front of a city bus. The people around me said I slipped off the curb and fell in front of it. That's how I got these cuts and bruises. If the gentleman who was standing next to me hadn't quickly pulled me back, I would have been hit head-on by the bus."

"Wow, do you know who the man is? I want to meet him and thank him for saving your life."

"No, I don't know him, but the police have talked to him. I'm sure they can give you his name and phone number. I'd also like to thank him."

"Next time, my love, please be more careful when you're standing on the corner waiting for the light to change. In fact, don't stand in the front row at all, but get in the middle or the back."

"I know, Sam, I've been thinking of that myself while lying here, And there's something else that's been bothering me. I'm sure I wasn't that close to the curb. I'm always careful about that, because with all of the people standing around so close together, I've always thought it could be dangerous."

"What are you saying, Barcelona?"

The tears started to fill her eyes again.

"Sam, I believe someone pushed me in front of that bus."

Chapter Twenty-Nine

I asked Barcelona how long she was going to be staying in the hospital.

"Not long, Sam. You know I have a performance tonight."

"Now you're the joker. You're not serious about going to the theater tonight and performing?"

"Of course I am. Remember what we people in the theater say: the show must go on. There are many people who've purchased their tickets months in advance, and I'm not going to disappoint them. After all, it's just a few scrapes and bruises. My clothing and the skills of the makeup department will cover them and no one will notice. Besides, if I *was* really pushed, I'm not going to let the one who did it make his or her wish come true. I'll go on tonight as if nothing happened. That's what a good actress does. The doctor said I've no other injuries, and I'm free to leave the hospital if I want to."

I could see I wasn't going to talk Barcelona out of it, so I told her I'd drive her to my office. She could rest on the couch and Donna would be there in case she needed anything. I had my appointment with the Chief and Donna had the phone number, and I could be back within fifteen minutes if she needed me.

I asked Barcelona to please give me a ticket for the performance for that night, because I wanted to be there and not let her out of my sight for too long. After the show was over and she was through doing the things she had to do, I would be taking her home with me and she would be sleeping in the guest room.

Barcelona agreed without hesitation, as she was still frightened about the bus situation, and her body was now kicking in with a little pain. She also reminded me that she had to be back at the theater no later than 7:15 that night.

And then she said with a big grin on her face, "About tonight, Sam. Me staying at your place. I know you won't take advantage of me."

I smiled back and jokingly replied. "Don't be too sure of that, Barcelona Jones. What you can be sure of is that I'll get you back in time for the show that must go on. My appointment is at five. I'll be back here at six-forty-five. That'll give plenty of time to get you to the theater for the evening performance."

I brought Barcelona to the office and introduced her to Donna. I gave her a blanket and a pillow. (I'd slept on that couch many times myself.) When Barcelona was comfortable, and before I left, I asked Donna to keep an eye on her. And if there was any change or Barcelona needed me, to call immediately if not sooner.

"Don't worry, boss, I'll watch her like a hawk watches her newborn chicks in the nest."

I leaned over and gave Barcelona a kiss on the forehead and then on the ... well you know where, and I was off to meet the Chief. Donna again had that quizzical look but said nothing.

This time I answered that look. "I'll explain it all to you when I get back from seeing the Chief."

I was sure that Donna would take complete care of my love, but still I hated to leave Barcelona. I knew that she was bravely putting up a good front. She was a great actress, but she wasn't fooling me.

Chapter Thirty

The Chief was waiting for me when I arrived at his office. We compared our notes, especially our talks with John Ashland the actor who had been in the hospital with the peanut allergy, and Mike Larson the agent. We found no discrepancies between the two separate interviews. We were still thinking that Larson was our killer.

The Chief said that he also liked Mike Larson immediately, just as I had. And for the life of us we couldn't come up with the motive of why he would want to kill off his clients, especially as all three were up for the lead in the movie, which meant he could make big bucks on whoever received the part. We even thought that maybe it was because he would make more commission from one of them than the other. That was a new thought of ours, but I must confess not a very good one.

"You know, Sam, maybe the murderer is a person we haven't thought of yet, like someone else in the play. Maybe Michael Sparks, the understudy, *was* the intended victim, and not John Ashland as we thought. I wonder if there's a third understudy who wanted a big chance on Broadway. Do you know who the understudy is now?"

111

"Sorry, Chief, I don't. But that's a great idea. Perhaps we've been barking up the wrong tree. I have a friend who's in the play. I'll ask her. I'm sure she'll know who it would be."

"Good, let's assemble the cast together and go over them with a fine tooth comb, and an open mind. Maybe something new will pop up. Also let's ask Mike Larson to be there. He may have some other actors under contract who are performing in *Murder on Broadway*. If so, I would like to know who they are."

I nodded. "I'll set up the time with my friend's help. I don't think there will be any problem. One of us can ask Larson if he has any other clients in the play. Either way, we tell him we'd like him to be there even if it's just to represent Ashland, and remind him that two of his other clients have been murdered. I'm curious to know if the new understudy is represented by him."

The Chief agreed. "Even though he's a very likeable character in my book, Mike Larson is still my number one suspect."

His voice was very firm when he said this. We had some small talk and he said he was sorry that he was unable to be at my parents' anniversary party. At the last moment he had another homicide case to attend to.

"Too bad, Chief. The party was great, and you missed meeting my date."

"Who is she, Sam? Is it this your friend who's going to help you set up our meeting with the cast members? Or is it the red haired beauty who plays the second female lead? Or how about that dark haired cutie? Come on, Sam, confess up who is she."

"You'll just have to wait a little longer. In the next

few days the world will know. Have patience, Chief, have patience."

"So mysterious. I'm putting my money on the red head. Maybe it's her or maybe not. But one thing I know for sure, it's not that lead actress, the knockout blonde. You couldn't be that lucky. No, it's definitely not Miss Barcelona Jones."

Chapter Thirty-One

I rushed back to my office, and I could hear laughter. I walked in quietly and saw the two women sitting on the couch and having a friendly conversation. It warmed my heart, because Donna was like part of the family – and soon Barcelona would be also.

They both looked up at me and smiled, greeting me at the same time. "Hi, Sam."

"Hi, you two. How are you feeling, Barcelona? You seem to have got your color back."

"A little better. Donna and I are having fun getting acquainted, and she's told me some great stories about when you were a little boy. I hear you were always a prankster, which seems to have got you into a lot of trouble. I'm happy you kept your funny sense of humor. By the way, I told Donna about us. I hope you don't mind. She swears to secrecy."

"I don't mind at all. In fact it makes me feel good that you told her. Are you ready to go? I told you I wouldn't make you late for the theater. We'll get there by seven-fifteen, just as I promised. In fact you'll be there a little before 7:00. I have a stop to make after I drop you off. I may be a little late to the theater, but don't worry, I'll be there and hopefully on time."

On the way to the theater I told Barcelona the

Chief's idea about assembling the cast, and asked her if she would help in putting it together. She said she would, and didn't think there would be any trouble, saying, "The cast really wants to get these murders solved. Ever since the shooting on stage there's been a dark shadow in each performance. I'm sure no one notices it as they watch each of us perform, but it's there."

"Barcelona, is there a new understudy for John Ashland's part?"

"Of course. There's always an understudy for all the major parts. There are many people in the cast who are prepared at any moment to take over if and when needed."

"Who's the understudy now?"

"It's James Thomas. He's young and good looking. Has a promising career ahead of him. He only has a small part in our production, but I can tell he'll go far if he hangs in and doesn't give up. Sometimes in this business even the most promising actors and actresses don't make it. They give up too soon if they don't get the breaks. But they need to go on. I was fortunate I got those breaks. You could say I was one of the lucky ones. When would you like me to help set up the time for the gathering of the cast members?"

"The Chief said anytime would be okay with him. Whatever day or time we can get them together, he'll be there, rain or shine."

"I'll talk to them right after the final curtain goes down on tonight's performance. Maybe sometime in the next two days would be best. Most of us are free in the late morning. Would that be okay?"

"That would be great. I'll tell the Chief."

We arrived at the theater at 7:00. I walked her to

116

the back door, kissed her gently on the lips, and started to walk away.

"Oh, Sam, I'll have a ticket waiting for you at the box office tonight. You can pick it up sometime after 7:30."

"Thanks, my love. You be careful. I'm sure you have an understudy too, so if at any moment you're not feeling well, please don't push yourself. Just let her do it."

"Sam, don't worry, I'll be fine. And my understudy is called Brenda Summers."

I hailed a taxi, gave him the address where I wanted to go and sat back in the seat. My words kept going over and over in my mind that I had said to Barcelona. "I'm sure you have an understudy too."

And her reply. "My understudy is called Brenda Summers."

Was it possible that Barcelona's understudy could be the one who pushed her in front of the bus? While thinking these things I realized that I'd forgotten to mention Barcelona's ordeal to the Chief.

I made a mental note to tell him before we met with the cast. This could give us another suspect, and we could watch the person more carefully while asking her questions. I had a tinge of panic thinking that Barcelona would be acting tonight, along with possibly the one who tried to kill her this afternoon.

I was hoping that the program of the performance would mention who the understudy was. I wanted to keep my eye on her. After all, there had been a murder in the play before, in front of a live audience, and there could be another murder tonight while I was watching. I came out of my deep thoughts when I heard the voice of the cabby.

117

"Here you are, buddy."

The taxi pulled over and stopped. I got out and was in front of a very fancy-looking jewelry store. My father swore by him, saying, "He's the best. Whatever you want made, he can make it."

After I explained to the jeweler my design he smiled, and said, "It will be very beautiful. She's certainly a lucky lady."

"No, actually *I'm* the lucky one."

On the way home I stopped off at the florist and bought one dozen white roses, with one red rose in the middle of the bouquet. I placed it in the guest room of my apartment where it would be greeting Barcelona when she walked in. My heart was fluttering with excitement just thinking that she was going to be sleeping there that night.

Chapter Thirty-Two

I arrived on time, picked up my tickets and all went well.

After the performance, I took Barcelona to my place. She was very tired, and the aches and pains from the accident were now strongly kicking in. When she went into the bedroom the first thing she saw was the roses. She looked over at me and moisture began to blur her eyes. She kissed me, and said, "Sam, you're such a romantic and I love it. And I love you even more. Thank you so much."

I gave her a pair of my PJs and she went right into the bathroom to change. The night's performance had taken a toll on her. When she came out she went straight to bed. I didn't argue, although I was hoping to have some conversation with her. I wanted to tell her of my love, even though I knew she already knew it. I couldn't help myself. Every chance I got I would instill my love to her.

As I stood in the bedroom doorway, Barcelona fell asleep very quickly right in the middle of my asking her about Brenda Summers, her understudy. I wanted to hear Barcelona's opinion of her.

I closed the door gently and tiptoed out of the bedroom and called the Chief. I told him about

Barcelona's ordeal that day in front of the bus, and her feelings that she believed she'd been pushed. The one thing I did get out of Barcelona before she fell asleep was that she had set up the cast meeting for the very next morning. She said they were all anxious to find out what was going on. The Chief told me he would be there, come hell or high water. I never did completely understand what that meant, and I still don't! I also told the Chief about my suspicion of Brenda Summers, Barcelona's understudy.

I had seen Brenda's name on the program for the performance that evening, which gave a glimpse of each of the characters in the play. This way I could watch her in her usual role whenever she was on the stage. I thought she had been very good in the second lead, which was a much larger part than I thought an understudy would have.

Later when I asked Barcelona about this, she said that sometimes the second lead would be ready to take over the main character's part at any time. It was this director's wish that all members in the cast should be able to take over a part at any moment's notice.

Friday

The next morning the Chief and I met outside the theater. He was obviously intrigued as to which actress I was dating, but he clearly wasn't going to ask me outright. He was probably going to use his powers of deduction!

First, we talked to the players, giving them an overall view of what was happening so far. We were careful not to mention the name of anyone who was a suspect, even though of course someone asked.

Then we asked for any information that they could give us, especially regarding the night that Anthony Sparks was murdered. For instance, did anyone see someone back stage that they had not seen before, or anything that might be of some help, no matter how small or irrelevant it may be.

That's when Brenda Summers spoke up. "I saw an older gentleman walking around. I'd never seen him before."

The Chief asked, "Can you describe him to us? What was he wearing? Was he young, old, white, black, Asian? Any help you can give us would be greatly appreciated."

Brenda thought for a moment, as though picturing the man in her mind. "He was aged about … sixty-five or seventy I think. White, and maybe in the neighborhood of six feet. He was bent over so it was hard to tell. He had grey hair and a darker mustache and beard. Dressed kind of shabby-looking with a floppy hat and beige coat. I remember at the time I wondered who he was and what he was doing back stage."

The Chief turned to the other actors. "Did anyone else see this person?"

Most of them shook their heads. I looked over at Barcelona. She smiled, shaking her head also.

This gave the Chief an opportunity to ask Miss Summers if it was possible that we could talk to her privately, to see what else she might remember about that fatal night and the mystery man she said she saw. I knew he wanted to pick deeper into her memory, to see if she could recall anything else.

She agreed, and the director who was there said we could use his office. We thanked him and the three of us adjourned there. Before we went inside, the Chief told the cast that he would not be long with Miss Summers, and for them to think about that night, and to talk to each other. Maybe someone else might have seen or heard something that would help us solve the case soon.

Brenda Summers was very attractive. She had bright red hair, and on her it looked extremely good. She was a little older then Barcelona, and very sure of herself, which gave her a strong personality. You either liked her or you didn't, and the thought was that she didn't care either way. You could tell that was okay with her.

I came right out with the question that was on my heart. "Miss Summers, where were you yesterday afternoon between eleven-thirty and twelve-thirty?"

She looked startled, as though not expecting that sort of question. "I'm not sure why you're asking me, but to make you happy I'll certainly answer it. I was at the theater getting a fitting."

"And did you see Miss Barcelona Jones there?"

"Of course. We were both getting a new outfit for the play, so the costume director and seamstress called us both in. They said it saved them time if both of us came in together."

"Did the two of you leave at the same time?"

"I think so. Yes. We walked out of the theater together. Usually we walk the same way, but this time Barcelona said that she was bringing lunch to someone, so we departed in different directions."

"Did you go straight home?"

She looked puzzled rather than upset by my questions. "I stopped for coffee, than realized I'd left a bag at the theater with some items I'd been using before the fitting. On the way back to the theater I met some fans. I walked with them for awhile, and we were talking so much that I passed up the theater."

The Chief broke in. "Who were the fans, and did you happen to see Miss Jones again?"

"If you're asking for the names of those people, I don't know them. They were just fans, not friends. As for Barcelona, I did see her again. I guessed she also stopped, because she had a couple of bags with her. I suppose it was the lunch she was bringing to the person she was meeting."

"Where did you see her?" This time I cut into the conversation.

"She was on the corner, waiting for the signal to change to cross the street. I looked away for a moment then when I looked back I heard screaming and I saw a crowd gathering. I assumed they'd recognized Barcelona and were getting her autograph and taking pictures. This happens quite often to her. She's a big star on Broadway. I didn't want to add more confusion so I went back to the theater, picked up my bag and went home. I didn't realize what had happened until Barcelona shared with me about falling in front of the bus. She and I are very good friends."

I was thinking to myself, *Neat cover-up, Miss Summers. You had to admit to being there, in case we can produce an* eyewitness. I knew she had had plenty of time to come up with a good alibi. Plus, I was thinking she could also have switched the stage gun for the real one that killed Anthony Sparks, and so was making up the story about the mystery man whom no one else had seen.

"One more question, Miss Summers," the Chief

was asking again. "Can you think of anything else about the older man you saw the night of the murder?"

She thought for a little while. "I think so. Yes, I can. I don't know why I hadn't thought of it before, but when I saw him he smiled, and I could see that two of his front teeth were missing. It was strange and was as if he wanted me to notice, because when he smiled at me he put his tongue between his missing teeth so I would see the space."

Chapter Thirty-Three

As Brenda Summers was leaving the director's office, the Chief asked her to please not tell anyone about our conversation, especially the part about the mystery man with the missing front teeth. She put her hand to her lips and sealed them off, as if she had an imaginary zipper, giving the motion of locking them with a key and then tossing the invisible key away.

When we were alone, the Chief said, "Well, it seems I was wrong. Your date is definitely *not* Miss Summers. She's not your type at all, so I guess it's the dark haired one."

I just smiled and said nothing.

"By the way, Sam, Mike Larson couldn't make it. He already had an appointment, but he did say he had no other clients in the show."

We went back to the cast members and asked a few more questions. Since we weren't getting anywhere, we told everyone to go home and rest for the night's performance. No one was to leave town, and some time if in the future we met them again, hopefully we'd be able to give them some solid information – or better yet, tell them that the case was closed.

After the Chief left, I walked over to Barcelona. I

thought she still looked tired. She asked me to take her home because she wanted to rest for a few hours before the curtain went up. I was disappointed, but knew it would be best for her. On the way to her home I asked if there was a time when the theater was ever empty during the day.

She said she thought that it might be empty for an hour or so during the day, but wasn't completely sure. "There's probably always someone there, but they could be anywhere, even taking a nap at any given time."

"Is the stage door always locked? And if so, how does someone get in if they want to come early?"

"The four leads have keys, but we seldom use them. I've only used mine once. It was late at night around twelve-thirty and I'd forgotten my manuscript. It was at the beginning of the run and the director had changed two pages of dialogue and wanted us to perform changes on the next performance. I found the theater very spooky when there's no one around."

"Remind me again: who are the four leads?"

"John Ashland, Brenda Summers, and now it's James Thomas since he's moved up – and of course me. This isn't always the case. I've been in some plays where no one has keys. But this director has many of his own ideas and he's one of the best. There's a good chance he'll be chosen to direct the movie. I hope he gets the go-ahead. He has a knack of bringing out the best from his players."

"James Thomas? Was he there this morning for the meeting? I don't remember seeing him."

"No, he didn't say what it was, but he was involved in something confidential today. Was kind of discreet when I asked him, so I left it alone. I'm not one who

126

likes to pry into other people's business."

"How about John Ashland? Was he there?"

"No again. He said he had an appointment with his agent, Mike Larson,"

I dropped Barcelona off and headed back to the jewelry store. The jeweler wanted to make sure that what he had done so far was to my liking.

The ring I designed had a diamond in the middle of around five karats, with two rows of seven diamonds on each side. I remembered when I was a kid I went to church and the pastor said that the number seven represented perfection, or being perfect – and that was what Barcelona was to me … perfect.

Chapter Thirty-Four

Saturday

The weekend was now upon us, which meant I would not get to see my true love. I went to the office on Saturday, going over my notes again.

Brenda Summers had now joined the small list of suspects, but I still had nothing tangible. I called the Chief for help but he was not in. I remembered that because it was Saturday he was probably spending the day with his family.

Thinking about family, I thought of the conversation I had with my folks the day before, when I called them to wish them a happy voyage.

Dad had answered the phone. "Hi, Sam, We were just heading out the door. Here's your mother."

"Hi, Sammy. I was just thinking about you. Thanks for calling."

"Hi, Mom. Have a great time. And again, congratulations, and be careful."

"Sammy, have you seen Barcelona lately?"

"Yes, the Chief and I are working on the theater murders together, so I see her often."

I still wanted to keep them in suspense until they returned, before announcing our engagement. I wanted to tell them in person and see their faces.

CHUCK ANTONE JR.

"Oh, I was wondering if it was more than that." There was disappointment in Mom's voice. I had an urge of weakness to tell her. I was beginning to feel bad ... but not that bad just yet!

So I said, "It *is* possible, Mom. Keep praying, but I have to go. I don't want to make the two of you late and miss the ship. I just called to say have fun and to take care of each other."

"We will, Sammy, we will."

After thinking about yesterday's phone call, I went back to my notes, looking for a loophole in one of the suspects' statements. Whoever the murderer was, I knew he or she was very sharp in hiding evidence.

I was so deep in thoughts when the phone rang I nearly jumped out of my seat. It was James Thomas, the new understudy for the male lead. He said he was sorry about missing the cast meeting the day before, and that he'd talked to Barcelona and she'd advised him to call me to set up an appointment. Of course this day was out, but sometime Monday morning around 11:00 would be good. We set the appointment up for that time here at the office.

I started to write down questions I wanted to ask him, especially if he'd seen the elderly man walking around backstage on the day of the murder. I was sure he hadn't, because I was convinced the man was just a figment of Miss Summers' imagination, to throw us off guard.

I lay on the couch in my office, took a long nap, and when I woke up it was dark. I walked home and on the way looked up at the marquee and thanked God for the woman's name that was on it in bold letters.

I stopped off for dinner. I was starving, and

130

believe it or not, still sleepy. By the time I got home I was ready for bed. I started to read the newspaper and promptly fell asleep.

I woke up very early the next morning, Sunday. Way too much sleep I guess. I fiddled around and had my usual breakfast, dressed, and headed to the little church I'd gone to before, to thank God for putting Barcelona in my life. The people again were friendly and welcoming. To my amazement they remembered me from the last Sunday when I was there.

There I was, sitting in a pew for the second straight Sunday. I actually was enjoying the service, even opening the hymnal and signing. My mother and father would have been so proud of me and so happy that I'd finally come back to the Lord – as they would say – and I was starting to believe that myself.

My thoughts went back to Barcelona. I was wondering what she would think about all of this. Then my mind went back to the singing which soon stopped as the pastor got up to give his message.

"Last Sunday we talked about thanking the Lord for giving you something or someone special. This morning my message is about loving that gift, and being completely satisfied with it."

I knew that again I was going to love the message.

Chapter Thirty-Five

Monday

I was happy when Monday arrived, because I was going to see the love of my life. We had made plans to meet for a late lunch at my place. I'd given Barcelona a key the night she slept there. I told her I'd call her just as soon as I was through talking to James Thomas, the understudy for the male lead.

He arrived on time, and turned out to be another of those likeable people. I guessed he was about eighteen. I remembered Barcelona saying he was young, handsome and talented. I didn't know anything about the talent part, but James was very handsome and, like I said, young.

I asked him if he would like to make the movie of *Murder on Broadway,* especially in the male lead. I was curious to see how badly he wanted the part.

He smiled. "I'd love to be in the movie, but when I went in to talk to the big guys they all said I was much too young to play the lead. I guess that looking young isn't always good. But I know when I get older I'll appreciate it. The real reason I wanted to talk to them was because I was hoping to play *any* character in the movie. I didn't really care how big or small the part was. I know this is going to be a very big movie and I want to be part of it."

"Did you see anyone wandering around the back stage the day of the murder? Someone you'd never seen before?"

He shook his head. "No, I don't recall seeing anyone. Is there someone special you're thinking of? If so, what did they look like? Maybe if I knew who it was I could be more help."

I described the man that Miss Summers said she'd seen, not mentioning the missing teeth, and asked him to think back to that day.

Again he shook his head. "I'm sure I didn't see anyone fitting that description."

"So, James, why couldn't you make the meeting on Friday morning?"

"My wife had a morning doctor's appointment that day."

I interrupted him. "Your wife? How old are you anyway? I thought you were about eighteen."

"I get that all of the time. I'm twenty-five, and I've been married a little over two years. We found out that my wife is carrying our first child and I wanted to go with her for her first appointment. We spent the rest of the day visiting friends and telling them of our blessings. If I'm a suspect of any kind, ask away with the questions. I don't mind."

"No need. And, James, *everyone* is a suspect at the beginning of every murder case. But you can be assured that if your alibi is confirmed, you're no longer one of them. I need the name and address of your doctor and the time of the appointment. Of course, the Chief Inspector on the case may want to ask you some further questions, but it will be just a formality."

After James Thomas left, I called Barcelona who was waiting for me at my place. When I had given her the key I told her she could use it at anytime, even when I wasn't there. It was walking distance from the theater and much closer than her place.

I stopped off at the florist and bought just one red rose. I knew she had a bouquet at her place, and also one at my home. But I wanted to remind her again of how much I loved her.

This time I put a card with it: *Each time you look at this rose, be reminded that my heart belongs to you.*

Chapter Thirty-Six

My heart was doing flip-flops again as I got closer and closer to my home. I knew Barcelona was there waiting for me. When I opened the door and walked in, a delicious aroma filled my nostrils.

"Hi, my love. Whatever you're cooking smells wonderful. I can't wait to indulge myself. It smells like Italian."

"Right you are, 'my soon-to-be-husband.' It's an old family recipe. Meat balls like you've never tasted before, and penne with just the right amount of spices in the sauce to tempt you to have more than just one helping."

I leaned over and kissed her and held her tight. I loved it that she said I was soon to be her husband.

"Barcelona?"

"Yes, Sam, what is it? You sound so serious."

"I've been wondering a lot about how you'll feel when you start telling your friends and the press about me. After all. I'm just a private detective, and you're a big star on Broadway. I'm sure you must be wondering what people will say. I mean, you could have married a prince or even a king or a millionaire."

"Actually, Sam, I've never thought about it. I just know that I'm madly in love with you. And that's all that matters to me. And, Sam, you're not *just* a private detective: you're a very good one ... the best! Besides, I heard through the grapevine that you make more money than I do."

"What grapevine was that?"

"Well, after the first day I came to your office, not only did I ask the Chief about you, but I made three or four phone calls to some of my influential friends." She smiled. "They all said you were extremely dependable. Either they, or someone they knew, had hired you in the past. Two of them said you and your father were, and are, very successful detectives. Expensive but worth it. Then they said that you probably made more money than I do."

With that, she turned around, her shoulders shaking in laughter. She stopped, looked at me and said, "Yes, I could have married a prince or a king, but I'll leave that up to Grace and Rita. Besides, it's you I love and want to marry."

Of course, that reference to royalty meant something to us both back then. The famous film star Grace Kelly had married Prince Rainier of Monaco in 1956 and Rita Hayworth married Prince Aly Khan in 1949, this being one of her five marriages. I knew I was only going to be married once.

I walked over to Barcelona, put my arms around her and gave her a great big long kiss. We held each other for a long time.

Finally Barcelona pulled away. "Let's eat, before my hard work of cooking for you for the very first time gets cold." She had a pleading look in her eyes. And by that look I knew she was saying: *This is dangerous, and until we get married let's not put ourselves in this kind of situation.* I held her hand as we walked to the table, and squeezed it as if to say *I understand.*

We spent a great time together, talking about our childhood again, our teenage years, and how and why we chose the profession we each had. We'd talked about it all before, but enjoyed it again, even thinking of other things we'd forgotten to mention. It was wonderful sharing our thoughts and our young life experiences. After all, we had met, fallen in love, and were almost engaged in less than two weeks.

Barcelona mentioned that the hot Hollywood star Charlie Long had flown back to New York to meet with all of the people involved in the making of the movie, and that John Ashland would also be there. The meeting was in the morning at 10:30, so it might be possible that we would not be able to see each other, because Barcelona had no idea how long the meeting would be. And of course she had the performance that night.

This was Monday, and the day after the meeting would be Wednesday, and we'd have the whole day together. She promised to call sometime after the meeting, and before the curtain went up in the evening, adding that maybe we'd have time for a quick cup of coffee in between, so I was surprised when the phone rang on Tuesday morning and I heard her voice.

"Hi, Barcelona, so you couldn't stay away from hearing my voice today, huh?"

"I love hearing your voice, Sam, but I'm calling to say we've just heard that Charlie Long is in the hospital. He's not doing well. He was run over early this morning. By a hit-and-run driver. He's in St. Ann's."

Chapter Thirty-Seven

I told Barcelona I'd meet her at St. Ann's Hospital. But just before I left, I called the Chief. I was pretty sure this hit-and-run was connected with the other two murders. He said he'd meet me there.

When I arrived at the hospital, Barcelona was waiting for me. She was talking with my sister Erica, who was on duty that day. Barcelona had already found out what room Charlie Long was in, so we went straight there.

Charlie was in a coma, with tubes coming from everywhere. Sitting in a chair next to Charlie's bed was a man who was unrecognizable to the two of us. He stood up and reached out his hand. "Hi, I'm Edward, Charlie's new agent."

"New agent?" I asked. "I thought Charlie was signing up with Mike Larson."

"He was about to, but since he never received the contract through the mail he called me and said he wanted someone to represent him who was living closer. I was the lucky guy he signed up with. If he survives this, he's bound to become the next big male star, especially if he gets well soon and is given the male lead in the movie with you, Miss Jones."

Barcelona said, "No decision has been made yet.

We were going to do that today at the meeting. Either way, I pray Charlie will come out of this and be able to resume his promising career."

The Chief had now joined us. I introduced him again to Barcelona and then to Edward. The Chief looked at Edward and lowered his voice. "Have the doctors given you any prognosis about Charlie Long's condition?"

"Not yet, but it doesn't look good. In a way I feel responsible. Charlie and I sat up last night talking about what the movie version of *Murder on Broadway* would do for his career. He was so excited about doing it, and working with Miss Jones. Around one o'clock this morning, he said he couldn't sleep and was going to go out for a walk.

"He asked me if I wanted to join him, but I said no, as I was too tired. We looked out the window of our hotel and saw that the streets were deserted. He said he wouldn't be long. I told him to be careful and hurry back so I wouldn't worry about him. He laughed and said, 'Don't worry; I have a feeling that things are going to turn out really good.'

"When he got outside of the hotel he looked back up at me. I was standing in front of the window. He waved and I waved back. I started for my bedroom and that's when I heard the awful sound of him screaming, and then the thud. I ran to the window, looked down, and saw what I knew was the body of Charlie lying there. I saw no car and no one in the area. As I ran out of the hotel I told the desk clerk to call an ambulance and say that someone had been hit by a car. That's all I know."

The Chief said, "It's not your fault. Don't even entertain that idea. If you do, it can swallow you up."

142

"Thanks, Chief, that helps a lot. I've been sitting here blaming myself, thinking if I had only gone with Charlie as he asked me to, this wouldn't have happened. He looks so pitiful lying here with all of these tubes in him. I'm afraid for him and his life. Even if he survives, what will he be like?"

Erica and another doctor came in. My sister took us outside the room and said quietly, "It doesn't look promising. We'll have to wait until he comes out of the coma before we get the big picture. What we do know is he has a broken right collarbone and a right leg fracture, along with some broken ribs. Those aren't too serious. But his spleen is messed up. The most serious injury is a blow to the skull causing swelling to the brain. If there's any brain damage we won't know until he wakes up. It could be today, tomorrow or even weeks or months. That is, if he wakes up at all."

Chapter Thirty-Eight

Barcelona had some appointments to keep before the performance that night, so she had to leave.

The Chief, Charlie's new agent Edward and I went down to the hospital café. As we sat down with our coffee and a snack, the Chief asked, "Edward, is that your first or last name?"

"First name. My family name is Oppenheimer. But I just go by Edward. It's so much easier."

"We would like to ask you a few questions, if that's okay with you."

"Of course. Go ahead, Chief."

"Who else knows that Charlie Long had signed up with you as his agent?"

"Well, it was no secret, especially among the biggies who would be at the meeting. I'm sure they all knew. That's why I'm here. If Charlie got the part, I would do the negotiating. If John Ashland got the part his agent, Mike Larson, would do the same. We weren't invited to the meeting, but afterwards the agent of whoever got the role would meet with all concerned for the signing of the contract."

"Do you know if Mike Larson was there?"

"Yes, he and I waited outside the office. We're

friendly, but our conversation wasn't anything special. Just small talk."

I asked the next question. "Did Mike Larson seem annoyed or angry that Charlie signed up with you?"

"Not at all. In this business we win some and we lose some. As for me, I can't worry about it and just try my best to represent the clients I have. Mike was surprised though. He said he'd sent the new contract to Charlie and wondered why he never heard back. I told him Charlie had mentioned that he never received the papers."

"Do you have some big name clients? Like someone we'd recognize?"

"I'm sure you would. They're mostly movie stars. If you want their names, it's no secret. I can give them to you."

"No. it's okay. It's not needed at this time. By the way, who did you feel was going to receive the part?"

"The scuttlebutt around was that Charlie Long had an in. Not sure why. Some said it was the choice of the director and the producer, and others said Charlie was Miss Jones' choice. She wanted to work with him, and she felt he was right for the part. But like I said, that's just hearsay.

"Being Charlie's agent, of course I wanted him to win. Personally, I believe that Miss Jones would have the final say, and I do believe she would have chosen Charlie Long. But Mike probably would say the same thing about his client."

"Thanks, Edward." The Chief was now speaking, "You've been a big help. How long will you be staying here?"

"Not sure. I called my secretary in Hollywood and told her to cancel all my appointments for the next two days. Didn't tell her why, as I wasn't sure Charlie's wife had been notified yet about the accident. I'd like to stay until the doctors can give us a more exact diagnosis. But the doctors said he could be in the coma for weeks or even months. Or longer. I have to return back to my other clients. I can't be away too long. I'm sorry about Charlie, but I have a responsibility to all my clients and the agency I represent."

"Of course," I said. "The Chief and I understand if you have to leave. If you like, we'll keep you posted."

The three of us went back up to Charlie's room, where he still remained in the comatose situation. Soon afterwards, the Chief and I left, both agreeing that our two prime suspects were Brenda Summers and Mike Larson. We were both leaning on Larson, but Miss Summers was not out of the picture yet.

We arranged to talk to each one again, listening for something we might have missed before. We now felt that both suspects had good reasons to commit the homicides.

Mike Larson, being the agent of John Ashland, would make big bucks if he'd gotten the part. And John Ashland's only surviving competition was Charlie Long. Now with him possibly out of the way, the part would be his. But the question was: Would Mike Larson commit murder to help his client?

As for Brenda Summers, she would probably be the number one choice for the movie's female lead if Barcelona was out of the picture. But why murder the other male leads in contention? Maybe Miss Summers was trying to throw us off, so we would suspect someone else – someone like Mike Larson and not her.

The Chief and I were pondering over the same questions. Was money, and a big part in a big hit movie, worth killing for? I had a feeling we were missing something.

Chapter Thirty-Nine

I was still not comfortable with Barcelona being out of my sight, not knowing what the killer would try next.

That evening, I slipped in through the backstage entrance. By now, most of the people knew who I was – not as the star's boyfriend, but as the detective who was working on the case.

I stood back in the wings where I could see all the action on the stage but not be seen by the actors. I didn't want Barcelona to notice me. I thought she might think I was there because there had been another murder, or because Charlie Long had died.

Every time Brenda Summers was onstage, I watched her with a pair of steel eyes, waiting for something to happen. ... Nothing did. I remember thinking how foolish I was, knowing Miss Summers would certainly not do anything as stupid as killing my love on stage. She would probably wait on some street corner where she knew Barcelona would be, and then give her a great big push in front of another bus. Then, unnoticed, nonchalantly walk away.

Chills went through my body as I wondered if there would be another attempt on my future wife's life. After the play, I came out of hiding. When Barcelona saw me she looked really surprised.

"Sam, how long have you been here? Is something wrong? Is Charlie okay?"

"As far as I know there's no change. Let's go get a bite to eat and I'll ask if I can use the phone there to call the hospital for a report."

We went to the small restaurant by where I lived. I called the hospital. Charlie was the same. The word was "No improvement."

I asked Barcelona about Brenda Summers, saying, "I've been thinking that if something happened to you, would Miss Summers take your place? Not only here in New York, but for the movie in Hollywood?"

"Sam, why would you ask that? Do you think Brenda pushed me in front of that bus?"

"It *is* possible, my love. I'm just grasping – looking for any reason why someone might want you out of the movie, or even out of this life."

Barcelona gave out a hearty laugh. "You can't be serious, Sam. Brenda and I are good friends. We've been together in other plays. She could be a star on her own if she wanted, but she likes doing the plays with me. We always have a great time together. In fact, she could have had this part, but she suggested me.

"She's happy being the co-star. She says that way there's no pressure on her. She loves to act, and tells me I can handle the pressure better than she can. She's a strange bird, I'll agree, but murder is *not* her forte. You either like Brenda or you don't. I happen to like her. She's honest and to the point. On the stage she's a great actress. Off stage she never acts, she's just herself. You always know where you stand with Brenda. And by the way, she's running for a Tony for best supporting actress. She's already won two, and she's the front runner to win another one this year.

"If I were you, Sam, I'd take Brenda off your list. It would be a waste of time to suspect her. But to answer your question, yes, she'd be the one who would most likely take over my part in the play *if* anything was to happen to me. And it would be very likely she'd receive the movie roll. She would definitely be my choice if for some reason I couldn't fulfill my contract."

I nodded. "Thanks. I'll take into consideration all you've told me, and relate it to the Chief. He'll probably still want to talk to Brenda, and so will I. But this time I'll look at her differently. If she's a friend of yours then I want her to be a friend of mine. But I have experiences of good and even best friends murdering each other. Please believe me, it does happen."

"Thanks, Sam. Give Brenda a good checkup. You'll find out she's overly honest and straightforward, which is why some people don't like her. But to me over the last few years she's been a really good friend. I hope she'll turn out to be your friend too. She'll be one of my bridesmaids, and possibly the maid of honor if my cousin from Washington State can't make it.

"My cousin is expecting to come, but because we haven't set a date yet, she's not sure if she'll be able to fly out here. She may be in the hospital having her baby. That's one thing about Brenda, she won't be insulted or have hard feelings if she's my so-called second choice. When we were young girls, my cousin and I promised we'd be each others' maid of honor. I was hers and she'll be mine if possible. And knowing her, she'll do her best to be here come rain or shine.

"I really would like to set the date for sometime after my cousin's baby comes. I think she's about four months pregnant. But I know Brenda will be delighted and honored to take over if she's needed at the last moment. That's the kind of person Brenda is. No, Sam, she is *not* a murderer."

I took Barcelona home, and on the way we made plans for the next day, her day off. I wanted to take her to the beach and amusement park at Coney Island.

Chapter Forty

Wednesday

We had a great day at Coney Island. I rolled up my pant legs and we walked the beach holding hands with the ocean water just above our ankles. Barcelona had on pedal pushers so she just pushed them up a little higher. Whenever a big wave came in she would let go of my hand and run toward dry sand. Then she would laugh, run back and grab my hand again. She looked so beautiful, as though she didn't have a care in the world.

We rode some of the rides, but the merry-go-round was our favorite. We each took a horse on the outside of the carrousel. Then each time we went around we took a large brass ring from the ring machine and tossed it into the monkey's mouth: a big cutout of a monkey with his mouth open. Whenever the ring went in, a loud bell would ring. Every time Barcelona hit the target she shouted out, "Another point for me!" I learned that day that she was very competitive – something else I loved about her.

We had lunch at a hotdog stand with all the trimmings. I had two, Barcelona one. But I could tell she wanted part of mine, so I divided my second one and gave half to her. She gave me that great smile.

"Thanks, Sam, you must really love me." Then she let out this little giggle.

"I do, my love, and until the day I die I will always give you all that I have, no matter what it may be. You will never have to ask. I will always be there for you."

The rest of the day was filled with great memories and we vowed we would go back to Coney Island again and again, even it was just to share a hotdog with all the works.

We did go back as much as possible, and when the kids were old enough to enjoy the rides and the beach and all it had to offer, we took them. We continued to go back at least once a year, but most often twice. Soon our children brought their children, it has become a tradition. We loved having our grandchildren there. The carousel has remained not only our favorite, but the favorite of all the family. We now keep score of the ring tossing and keep adding to it every time we all go.

I arrived home after 9:30 that night. I took Barcelona home first because she was tired out. We both agreed that we had a day that we would always remember. I called the Chief at his home to tell him what Barcelona had said about Brenda Summers. Just as I thought, he said he still wanted to talk to her and to Mike Larson. He asked if I was available the next day. I told him I had an early appointment with a new client but was free all afternoon.

Then he said, "Well, if Miss Summers is really that nice of a person, maybe *she* is your new girlfriend. I'm going to watch the two of you closely when I question her tomorrow. I'll call you some time after lunch and tell you what time the two appointments are. And, Sam, I hear you laughing. Are you pulling my leg? Is there really a new lady in your life?"

I gave no answer, and after we hung up I went right to bed but couldn't sleep. My thoughts were on the day and how fortunate I was to be in love with Barcelona. And how super-fortunate I was that she was in love with me.

Chapter Forty-One

Thursday

I got up extra early the next day, walked to the office, and stopped on the way for breakfast. I was actually excited to talk to Brenda Summers. I now had a whole new look about her, especially after hearing the positive comments from Barcelona. I was hoping by the time the questions had ended, I too would have found a new friend, and not a murderer.

Donna hadn't arrived, so while I waited I went through the files of a new client, and then I looked over my notes from the two initial interviews of Mike Larson and Brenda Summers. I kept thinking that maybe I had missed something before. I went over the two interviews in my mind, hoping something would pop into it – something that I hadn't written down that might help us. But again I got nothing.

I was thinking that maybe today one of them would slip up and reveal a new clue, when the phone rang. It startled me, I was so deep in thought. It was the Chief. "Hi, Sam, glad you're there. Is this a good time to talk to you?"

"Yea fine, Chief. What's up?"

"I hope you don't mind but I made the two appointments for today to meet in your office? I felt the two would be more relaxed there than at my office at the police station. Mr. Larson will be there at one, and Miss Summers at three. How are those times with you?"

I told him that would be fine with me. He said he would see me around 12:30 in the afternoon for a preliminary discussion – if that was okay. I said that it was.

When Donna came in I told her about the meetings, and she asked if she should leave. I said no, it would be all right for her to stay.

Around 12:15 p.m. there was a gentle knock on my door. I knew it was Donna. She had a special way of knocking that always alerted me that she was coming in.

"The Chief is here, and I'm going to make a fresh pot of coffee." She came back with pastries she had bought from the bakeshop downstairs.

The Chief followed close behind. We greeted each other, and again went over our notes together. Then I read his and he read mine, and discovered they were very much the same.

The Chief said, "Now that we have them pretty much memorized, and they're fresh in our minds, we can both look for some discrepancies while we talk to our two suspects."

I agreed with the Chief that looking them over just before the questioning was a good idea, even though I had my notes down pat.

"Okay, we still have a few minutes before Larson comes in, so let's talk about this mysterious girlfriend of yours."

I was saved by the bell. Before I could say anything, Donna's voice came over the intercom. "Mr.

Larson is here for his one o'clock appointment."

He had arrived fifteen minutes early. I looked over at the Chief and gave him my best little smirky smile. "Please send him in."

The Chief and I both stood up and welcomed the very charismatic agent, Mike Larson. Before he sat down he went over and poured himself a cup of coffee and took a pastry. "Hope you don't mind, but I didn't have time for lunch."

"No, not at all." I was remembering his previous visit to the office when he also got his own coffee. His confidence was overflowing and I was again wondering if that was who he truly was – or was he putting on a show for us? Either way I was thinking that this man was probably a very good agent in making deals for his clients.

Chapter Forty-Two

Again Mike Larson was dressed meticulously, and even his teeth looked perfect. I wondered if they were real.

I asked him if and when he had sent the contract to Mr. Long. He said he *had* sent it but it was returned to him a few days ago. Apparently the wrong address had been put on the envelope. The Chief asked if he still had it. He said no, he'd thrown the contract away, because he'd heard through the grapevine that Charlie Long had signed up with someone else.

I was wondering how convenient that was. If he could have shown us the envelope, saying "return to sender" because of wrong address, that would have been helpful – and even maybe have helped to clear Larson a little. But now it still made him our number one suspect.

The Chief asked Larson if he'd heard about the hit-and-run on Charlie Long. He said he had, as he was at the meeting with Long's new agent, waiting for the decision on who would receive the part. And that was when they were told that he was in the hospital from a hit-and-run.

I asked, "Where were you last night at the time of the accident?"

"Like all normal people, I was in bed sleeping."

"May I ask, were you alone?"

Larson looked over at the Chief who had asked the question, then turned to look at me. "No I wasn't, but I'm not giving you anybody's name at this time." Then he broke out laughing. "Sorry, gentleman, I couldn't resist it. I was in bed with my wife. You can check with her if you like."

The Chief said in a grumpy voice, "You can be *sure* we will do just that."

In both of our previous conversations with Mike Larson he had never mentioned that he was married. I was thinking that was a little strange, and wondered why. So we weren't certain if it was true or not. I was thinking that maybe Mike Larson was pulling our legs to stall us off for awhile, so he could come up with a better alibi, and then tell us he was joking and had no wife. We also thought that the thing about the wrong address just didn't seem like him. He was too perfect to make a mistake like that. We both agreed it just wasn't his character – at least not the one he was trying to make us believe he was.

He left the office, still our prime suspect.

Chapter Forty-Three

Brenda Summers arrived right on time. Not a minute early or a minute late. The grandfather clock in the outer office had sounded its first bong as she walked in. Donna had been rearranging the pastry counter so the door to my office was open, and we could hear the chimes plainly. This clock was truly a grandfather clock, as it belonged to my dad's father, my grandfather, and had been part of our décor for many years. My daughter Lisbon who now runs the agency calls it the great-grandfather clock.

Miss Summers walked in looking every inch the Broadway star she was: hat, gloves, shimmering dress and of course, shoes to match.

She extended her hand to us as if she was the one who was going to do the questioning, as though she expected to be in charge the moment she entered my office. She sat down without being asked, crossed her legs, took out a cigarette holder, put a cigarette into it and waited for one of us to light it for her.

Neither the Chief nor I smoked, so we had no match. She reached into her purse, pulled out a cigarette lighter and handed it to the Chief.

He took it with a not-so-happy face and fumbled to light it. While doing that, Miss Summers opened up her purse and put the holder and cigarette back into it.

The Chief and I looked at each other and then at her. She looked up at us and started to laugh. "I don't smoke either. This is from one of the plays that I won my first Tony for, many years ago. It was about a murder similar to this one.

"Actually, Barcelona told me to do this. She thought that you, Sam, would get a big kick out of it. She said you had a great sense of humor. I hope I didn't embarrass the two of you. It was just playacting. But I can see by the look on your faces it wasn't such a great idea ... I'm very sorry."

We gave no comment and the Chief was not looking happy as he walked over and sat in the chair opposite Miss Summers. I walked over and sat in the chair behind my desk. Both the Chief and I didn't know what to make of the entrance we had just witnessed. I broke the silence. "You really had us fooled. Barcelona has given you a very good recommendation, telling us you're a very special friend of hers."

Brenda Summers didn't smile, but looked like she was hoping she could come in again and start all over.

I was wondering if Barcelona had told her about our relationship. She gave no sign that she knew that soon we were getting engaged. I was also wondering what the Chief thought about all this, considering he was more on the serious side while working on a case. And I didn't blame him. ... Murder is no fun.

The Chief broke my thoughts when he asked, "Miss Summers..."

She interrupted his question. "Please, Chief, call me Brenda." Then looking at me, "You too, Sam."

164

The Chief cleared his voice. "If you don't mind, while on this case I'll refer to you as Miss Summers."

Brenda smiled and nodded as if to say, I understand. She had a look of sadness on her face. I was beginning to feel sorry for her.

The Chief continued, "Miss Summers, we're wondering about the man you saw on the night of the murder of Anthony Sparks. Can you tell us anything more about him?"

"No, I'm sorry but I don't think so. I told you just about all I can remember. I've been thinking and going over it again and again in my head, but nothing new pops up. Why, did someone else come forward that saw him and mentioned something I didn't see?"

"No, nothing like that, Miss Summers. You're the only one so far who's seen him. We do wonder why no one else has come forward – if there was truly such a man." The Chief's voice had a slight edge to it.

"So you think I'm lying about this person I saw? I can assure you, gentlemen, I *am* telling you the truth."

I asked, "Brenda, tell us again what time it was, and were there many other people around?"

By now she wasn't happy and got on the defensive side. "I've said all of this before, so if you don't believe me then that's your problem. But I know what I saw. If you want, I'll tell you again."

We said nothing, and Brenda took our silence as approval for her to continue.

"I usually arrive about an hour early as most of the cast do. But that evening I went a little earlier, about six-fifteen. As you know, the performance starts at eight. I was thinking about that coming over here. Whoever changed the bullets must have known that the prop man always puts the blanks in the gun about two hours before curtain time. So whoever it was must have been there when I arrived, maybe waiting in some dark corner for the opportunity to change the bullets. Maybe even the mysterious man that *I* saw."

She emphasized the word *I*, paused for a short time, and then continued. "You know, the mysterious man you don't believe in."

There was no smile on her face, and I was thinking, *Maybe you were the one changing things.*

Miss Summers said, "Being that I arrived early, there was just mostly the setup crew preparing for the different scene changes. They're backstage with the equipment. We hardly ever see them. So I guess you could say I arrived an hour and forty-five minutes early. And no, there were not too many others there – to answer your question, Sam."

I could tell she was hurt and it revealed another side of her personality ... a softer side. Even though she was still on my guilty list I was seeing a different side of Brenda Summers, perhaps the side that Barcelona saw and liked. But that still didn't mean she wasn't capable of murder.

The Chief asked the next question. "So, Miss Summers, what happened after you saw the *alleged* man?"

Her voice rose a little higher. "He is *not* an alleged man." She again paused, then took control of herself. "I went straight to my dressing room, relaxed for about twenty minutes, and then changed my clothes. Soon after that I could hear the other players arriving."

"Did you think about the person you saw at all during that time?"

"No, Sam, I did not. I had no idea that there was

166

going to be a murder that night."

I looked at her and wondered if she was playacting or telling the truth. She had just showed us her acting ability when she made her entrance into my office, and it had been very convincing.

The Chief stared at her for a few seconds. "Okay, Miss Summers, thanks for coming in. We may want to talk to you again. And if anything comes up, please let us know."

"I will, Chief. And again I'm so sorry about the way I came into the office. I know this is a serious situation. It's just that Barcelona and I thought it would be fun. It wasn't, so please forgive me."

"Don't worry about it," I broke in. "You really had us fooled. You're a very good actress. Have you told anyone about the missing teeth? "

"No, of course not. You asked me not too."

As Brenda Summers left the office the Chief looked over at me. "How does Barcelona Jones know what kind of sense of humor you have?"

"Well, as you know, she's my client, and we've gone to places together like the hospital to interview John Ashland, the male lead actor, when he had the allergic reaction to peanuts. We've even had lunch together. Strictly business. I guess my sense of humor just pops up here and there."

The Chief gave me a sly smile. I was curious about his thoughts, but he asked no questions.

"You know, Chief, there *is* someone we haven't talked to yet who might shine some light on the investigation."

"Who's that, Sam?"

"The actor who actually pulled the trigger that fatal night."

"You're right. Sam. Why didn't we think of him before? Do you know his name?"

"Not offhand, but I do have a program for one of the night performances around here somewhere."

I fumbled around. I had just seen it that morning while cleaning up my desk. "Oh, here it is. His name is Kim Suzuki."

"Here's his picture. Just a thumbprint, but I recognize him from the play."

"I wonder if he knows about the fugu fish and how powerful the poison is. Could he possibly be one of those brave souls that take chances on their lives while eating it? Maybe he knows where one can buy such a fish."

"I don't know, Chief, but I thought at the beginning of this case that the one who actually pulled the trigger that night couldn't possibly be the murderer."

"You're right, Sam. Let's call him in."

Chapter Forty-Four

When I got home there was a message on my answering machine. This was, of course, one of the early tape devices, far different from today's digital models. The message was from Barcelona. She was at the hospital, and Charlie Long's wife had arrived.

Barcelona said she would be spending the rest of the day with Mrs. Long, and after the play they would both be spending the night at the hospital where arrangements had been made. Barcelona wanted to stay so she could comfort Charlie's wife the best she could, and she'd call me in the morning.

There was still some leftover dinner from Monday night that Barcelona had prepared, so I warmed it up. It seemed to taste more delicious than the night we ate it. I always did like leftovers. When I was through I stretched out on the couch and promptly fell asleep.

I was dreaming about calling Barcelona, when I woke up with my phone ringing. I got to it just before the answering machine went on.

"Hi, Sam, this is Marty." I could always tell if the Chief was calling from his office or at home, or some other place. From the office it was always "Chief," otherwise it was "Marty."

"Hi, Marty, what's up?"

"I've fixed an appointment to see Mr. Kim Suzuki tomorrow at my office. I'm checking with you to see when's a good time for you. Is the morning or the afternoon best?"

"So far, my day is free. I do have a few calls to make but I can make them any time. What's best for Mr. Suzuki?"

"He said he would prefer morning. He has the play tomorrow night. So how about ten? Does that sound all right for you?"

"It sounds good to me. Unless you call me, I'll see you at your office at ten."

Chapter Forty-Five

Friday

I arrived at the precinct station the same time as Kim Suzuki. In his late twenties, he was very cordial and didn't look like a killer. But not many do. The Chief introduced me as Private Detective Jones. We sat in the chairs facing the Chief's desk. He occupied his desk chair. I looked around. There was no coffee or pastries available.

"Mr. Suzuki, please tell us a little bit about yourself."

"Well, Chief, as you can tell I'm from an Asian background and, by my last name, Japanese. I was born right here in New York City twenty-seven years ago. Not married yet but very close. I went to university here in the city and graduated with a degree in criminology. Number two in my class."

With that he looked over at me. "If you ever need any follow-up work, Detective Jones, I'm your man. My specialty is chasing down information for cases where the boss has no time. Send me off anywhere in the world and I'll find out exactly what you're looking for."

171

I was thinking to myself that is the kind of guy I needed, someone to do all of the dirty work that I didn't have time for.

The Chief asked, "If that is your forte, what are you doing acting on Broadway?"

"I got bit by the acting bug when I was getting my degree, and it's fun. This part that I'm doing came up, not many lines. I'm only in the first act and the last. The pay is good, so I took it. Plus, I still have free time to do my real job."

I was curious, so I asked him, "Who are you working for? Maybe I know them."

"Right now I am working for the law firm Bradley and Sons Company. They're letting me investigate the case I'm on at my own time, just as long as I have all the info they need by the tenth of next month. I've worked for them once before. They're a nice group of people."

"Yes, I know of them. A very up-and-coming law firm. How long is your contract with the play?"

"It's for one year, and it'll be up in just over three months. If I decide not to renew it, or they don't want me any longer, it will be easy to fill my shoes."

Then looking directly at me, "Of course, I've heard of you, Mr. Jones. Actually I sent an application to you about four months ago asking for a job, but I've not heard back. I still have my hopes up though. I always say no news is good news."

"I'm sorry, I haven't been looking for anyone, but I'll check it out. I'm sure my secretary has it filed away somewhere."

The Chief was looking a little annoyed, as the actor had interrupted our conversation. He said, "Mr. Suzuki, the reason we called you in was to ask you some questions about the night Mr. Sparks was murdered."

"Yes, of course. I feel really bad that I was the one who pulled the trigger. I've been wondering why you haven't called me in before. Ask away and I'll answer whatever I can, but be aware I don't know much."

The Chief continued with the questions. "Was there anything different about the gun that night? Like was it in the same position as the other nights? Did it feel any different and did you see anyone wandering back stage that didn't look familiar?"

"No, I didn't see any unfamiliar faces that night. As for the gun, it's always on the table and in the same position. The handle is always facing toward me, making it easy to pick up so there is no dropsy's. Everything each night has to be the same, so all will work smoothly. That night was no different than any other night.

"Whoever changed the bullets knew the gun had to be placed in the same position, so all would be the same and the scene would go off without a hitch. That's why I think it was one of the players."

"One of the players? Is there someone on the set that you know of that has a thing against either Anthony Sparks or John Ashland?"

"No, not Mr. Sparks. Everyone really liked him. He was always encouraging to us smaller players. Mr. Ashland, now that's a different story. Besides whoever changed the bullets knew the gun had to be placed on the table with the handle out. Only another player would know that."

The chief continued with his line of questions. I was just sitting back, listening and getting to like Kim Suzuki more and more as he answered the Chief's questions. I could tell that he would really do a good job of investigating. He appeared to be very observant of the things that surrounded him, just as a good detective should do on a job.

"Mr. Suzuki, what do you mean when you say Mr. Ashland is a different story? What do you have in mind?"

"Truthfully, Chief, many of the players don't like him, including me. I've been observing the situation and there are a few players and crew who aren't too sad that Mr. Ashland almost died of that peanut poisoning. Anyone of them could be the murderer. Right now, there are two I'd ask about their relationship with Mr. Ashland. One is the new understudy, James Thomas. He's really nice guy, but he has some issues with Mr. Ashland."

"And the other one?" asked the Chief.

"I would really focus on Brenda Summers. She's very outspoken, and the two have butted heads together often. I'm not saying one of them is the murderer, but they may be able to shed some light onto the investigation. I'm sure they've talked to others in the play, and have more to say than they've told you so far."

"Well, that's about all I have. How about you, Sam. Any more questions?"

"No, Chief. What you've asked were the things I also wanted to know."

"Okay, Mr. Suzuki, you're free to go. If you have any new ideas that may help us, please let us know."

He smiled. "I hope I've been some help."

As he walked out he shook my hand and reminded me to look up his application for the job. I said that I would, and I actually meant it.

As the Chief's office door closed, I said, "I've already talked to James Thomas. He's a nice guy. He has a baby face, is married, and expecting their first child. In my book no one can be more innocent than he. But Brenda Summers, that's another story. I'm not sure of Miss Summers at all."

Chapter Forty-Six

Just as soon as I got home I called Barcelona, but there was no answer. I thought perhaps she was still at the hospital with Charlie Long's wife, Rachel, so I decided to go there. The weekend was coming up which meant I would probably not get to see her. But if I was lucky and did, it would only be over a quick cup of coffee.

When I walked into Charlie's room there were smiles on Rachel and Barcelona's faces. It appeared that there had been some movement from the patient.

When Rachel had come in and held his hand she had felt it twitch, and there was blinking of the eyes even though they were closed. The doctor said that was a good sign, as it appeared Charlie's brain was active and he most likely recognized his wife's voice.

Just about that time, my sister Erica came in. Her report was that the doctors had agreed that there had been some improvement, and within the next forty-eight hours they expected more. They felt this was a turning point, and an encouragement that it was possible that Charlie could come out of the coma within that time.

Erica then advised Rachel to continue to talk to her husband while holding his hand, since there seemed to be some recognition of who she was.

Barcelona and I went down to the hospital cafeteria. She looked tired and said she had to leave shortly as she needed to go home and rest. She also had to prepare for the night's performance. I asked her if she wanted to rest at my place, she said no, it was better that she went to her place and be alone. I understood, even though I wanted to spend more time with her.

We went back upstairs to Charlie's room. When we walked in there was an even bigger smile on Rachel's face. She said she'd been talking to Charlie while holding his hand, and she was sure he knew her voice.

Barcelona went over and gave Rachel a big hug and explained she had to leave to get ready for the night's show. "I may not be able to come by for the next two days, Rachel. I have double performances, but I'll try. Sam will keep me informed by telephone if we also don't get to see each other."

Rachel thanked Barcelona for staying with her the previous night at the hospital. She said she so appreciated it, and didn't know what she would have done, being there alone. She told Barcelona to be sure to go home and rest. The night before, they both had stayed awake most of the time watching over Charlie, getting very little sleep.

Chapter Forty-Seven

Saturday

When I woke up on Saturday morning I wrote a list of some of the things I wanted to get done before the day was through.

1. Read over Kim Suzuki's job request.

2. Call the jewelers to see if Barcelona's engagement ring is ready. (I was hoping to give it to her on the following Wednesday, her day off.)

3. Send a telegram to my folks telling them about the engagement. (I had intended to wait until they returned, but was afraid by that time the news media would have already told the world. And I wanted them to hear it from me.)

4. Go to the hospital to see how Charlie is doing.

I got dressed and went to the office where I hunted and hunted for the Suzuki application but couldn't find it anywhere. I finally called Donna at her home. She remembered reading it and said to give her a few minutes. She said she'd call back with the information I needed. About fifteen minutes later she walked into the office.

I told her she didn't have to come in. Since it was her day off, she could have just told me on the phone how to find it. Her reply was, "It's easier to come in and find it than to tell you where and how to look for it."

As she handed me Kim Suzuki's application she said, "I remember reading this and thinking that this is just the kind of person you need around here. What made you think of him?"

"I met him yesterday. He's the one who pulled the trigger that killed Anthony Sparks in the theater. I was very impressed by him. He said he sent a form looking for a job here but hadn't heard back. I told him I'd check it over. Now go home or do whatever you do on your day off."

Laughing she said, "Shopping. That's one of my favorite things. See you on Monday, unless you need to find something else. If so, just give me a call." She was still laughing as she left the office.

I checked over the application. It was well written with detailed information on Kim Suzuki, and on what kind of a job he was looking for. I decided to call him on Monday, since I knew the next two days were busy for him, and have him come into the office. I had recently been having second thoughts about needing someone else to help out, so I thought I would call Kim and offer him a job after he finished the one he was working on. I was excited just thinking about working with him. After reading his resume I felt we would work well together and make a good team.

I called the jeweler to see if the ring was ready. He said it was, and that it was one of the most beautiful settings he had made so far. He was closing at noon as it was the weekend, but would stay later if I wanted to come in that afternoon to pick it up. I told him no, it was okay, and that I would go in on Monday to settle the account and pick up the ring.

Next on my list was sending the telegram to my parents. I didn't want to write Barcelona's name, as I knew others would be reading the message. So after much thought I wrote, "Mom and Dad, your prayers have been answered. B.J. and I are getting engaged on Wednesday. Hope you're having a great voyage. Love to you both, Sam."

When I walked in Charlie Long's room in the hospital, my sister Erica and two other doctors were having a conversation with Rachel who was in tears. I quickly looked over at the bed thinking that maybe Charlie had passed away.

Even though tubes where still attached to him, Charlie looked over at me and gave a slight grin. I couldn't believe it. The doctors motioned to me by placing their index fingers to their lips and shaking their heads, indicating that they didn't want me to converse with him.

When they were through, Erica walked over to me and said, "It *is* a miracle. Sam. We were just telling Mrs. Long that we've never seen anything like this before. Charlie has a long way to go for complete recovery, but it looks mighty good. Right now, we're going to restrict his visitors, So, Sam, I'm sorry but you'll have to leave."

As I started out the door, Rachel came over to me

and we both hugged. "Please, Sam, tell Barcelona about Charlie. She's become such a dear friend and I know she'll be elated to hear the good news about my husband. When I thought I was going to lose Charlie, and the tears were flowing from my face, Barcelona reminded me of Alfred Tennyson's words that he wrote. 'Tis better to have loved and lost than never to have loved at all.' Those words were really comforting to me and I knew she was right. The best thing that's ever happened to me was falling in love with Charlie."

The tears came back into her eyes, but this time there was a smile on her lips as she looked over at her husband, knowing that this wasn't the end.

Many years later Barcelona also reminded me of the British poet's words when I lost my mother and father. I too found them encouraging and so very true.

I told Rachel that as soon as I left the hospital, I would go directly to the theater and try to relate the great news to Barcelona.

I walked out the room with my sister Erica, who said, "Please, Sam, don't take it personally about visitors not being able to see Charlie Long at this time. We just want to be cautious."

"No, I'm not at all offended. I'm just amazed. I'm sure he recognized me. I'll be heading right to the theater to tell Barcelona the good news, and about the restricted visitors. Do you think we can both come by on Monday sometime to see Charlie?"

"It may be possible, but please call first."

We were standing in front of the elevator. When the doors opened I stepped in, holding the doors so they wouldn't close. "Okay," I said, "I'll call first. By the way, here's a copy of the telegram I sent Mom and Dad."

182

Before Erica could open the envelope, I released the elevator doors, leaving her looking very confused as they were closing. I had to smile to myself as I wondered what she would be thinking while reading it.

Chapter Forty-Eight

Sunday

I was able to see Barcelona after I left the hospital, giving her the good news about Charlie Long. We agreed we would meet on Monday for a quick lunch and then head over to the hospital if the doctors said it was okay for Charlie to have visitors.

I woke up on Sunday morning and found myself getting dressed for church. By now I was calling it "My little church." As I walked in the church door everyone again greeted me with firm handshakes, and even some gave me hugs, welcoming me back.

The title of the message on the sign outside read, WHO CAN WE PRAY FOR TODAY?

After the greetings I was handed a piece of paper asking me to write down a name of the person I would like the church to pray for. Of course, my first thought was Barcelona, but the name I wrote down was Charlie Long.

After the service the pastor came over to me and invited me to have lunch with him and his family. Since I had nothing else to do, I told him I'd be happy to join him. It sounded great, and I asked where we were going. He said we would be going to his house. He assured me that even though lunch would be simple, the fellowship would be great.

Their home was connected to the church. I guess one would call it a parsonage. Anyway, it was small but very neat and homey. The pastor and his wife had three boys, all teenagers. It was a good family and I could tell that love was abundant to all. In many ways it reminded me of my growing-up days in our household. After we ate, the pastor said it was now getting-acquainted time. And with that, we all moved into the living room area.

The three youngsters shared first, then the pastor's wife, then the pastor. The pastor talked about his family and how they had come to the church where he had been the pastor for almost two years. When he started, there were about fifty in attendance and now there was a little over one hundred and twenty-five. He said he loved it there and loved the people who were all so welcoming to him and his family from the first day they arrived. He explained that being Africa Americans, that wasn't always the case.

When he was through, he turned to me. "Sam, are you married? Are you new to the area? And how did you come to us? I believe this is your third time here on a Sunday. Please tell us something about yourself."

I looked over at the teenagers, not sure if I wanted to talk about the murders and about Barcelona. The pastor caught my hesitance and excused the boys. They were due to go to youth meeting back at the church that was starting shortly. The pastor's wife thought maybe I didn't want her there either, so she got up to leave. I said that it was all right and for her to please stay.

"First of all, many thanks for inviting me to lunch. You have a great family. It reminds me very much of my family while I was growing up. To answer some of your questions, I'm not married yet, but very close.

"This coming Wednesday I will be officially engaged. We're not living together, in case you're wondering." Why I said, that I have no idea. I remember feeling a little embarrassed as soon as it came out of my mouth. "I'm not new to the area. I was born not far from here. I'm a private detective and working on a murder case that's been in the paper just about every day with the tag 'Murder on Broadway.' That's why I was hesitant for the boys to be here."

The pastor's wife spoke. "Yes, I've been reading about it." Then turning to her husband, she said, "It's the one about that Broadway star, Barcelona Jones."

He nodded. "Oh, that one. We have jokingly said that maybe she might be the murderer."

I was taken aback for a second, wondering how many others might be thinking the same thing.

"I can assure you Barcelona Jones is *not* the killer." My voice was a little stronger and a little louder than I wanted it to be.

The pastor said, "I'm sure she's not, but the paper and news programs leave everything to your imagination. We have no real thoughts about it." Then changing the subject, he continued, "How did you come to our little church?"

"I was walking past it and the message on the marquee – I guess I can call it that – said, 'Today's sermon will be being thankful.' It was just what I was looking for."

"And what were you being thankful for?"

"The girl I'm going to marry."

The pastor surprised me with the next question, "Is it Barcelona Jones, Sam?"

I looked over at both of them, then smiled. "Yes it is. How did you manage to come up with her name?"

"By the way you said her name. There tenderness about it. And then being so quick in defending her as not the murderer."

"Please don't mention this to anyone. I would rather it didn't leave this room until after the press get a hold of it."

"Don't worry, Sam. My wife's and my lips are sealed."

I ended up telling them the whole story of how I met Barcelona and fell in love with her the moment I saw her. We all laughed when I said it took her longer – about five days."

By the end of our time together not only did I share my life, but so did they in much more detail than they had before. By the time I left I felt I'd found two more special friends, and found the reverend who I was hoping would marry Barcelona and me.

Chapter Forty-Nine

Monday

I got up early on Monday morning and headed right for the jewelry store. The ring was beautifully made and looked exactly like my design. I was not disappointed at all. I wanted Wednesday to get here so I could give it to Barcelona, see the approval on her face, and become officially engaged. Then the rest of the world would know of my love for her, and I would be free to tell my family and friends.

I thought of the Chief and what his reaction would be, especially since he was so sure that it wasn't going be the star of *Murder on Broadway*.

The jeweler was about to put the ring into a velvet-lined square box, when I said, "No thanks. I'm going to look for a heart-shaped box."

"You don't have to look any further, Mr. Jones. Hold on for a second."

The jeweler disappeared for a few moments, and when he returned he was carrying two heart-shaped boxes. One was red velvet, the other black velvet with an embossed red rose on its top. I guess you can figure out which one I took.

I hurried home and called Mr. Suzuki. He was not in, and had no answering machine for me to leave a message.

I must have looked at the ring a hundred times while waiting for the time when I could pick up my love. At one point I even thought about giving it to her at lunch that afternoon, but I was hoping for a more romantic occasion than a quick lunch.

When the time came for me to leave and pick up Barcelona, I put the ring in my pants' pocket, but had second thoughts as I knew if I took it with me I would probably become weak and end up giving it to her immediately. So I took it out of my pocket and left it on the table. I was so anxious to put it on her ring finger and become engaged.

After we had lunch I called my sister Erica and asked if by any chance we could come over and see Charlie. The answer was a yes. Charlie had improved greatly over the last two days. The staff at the hospital were still overwhelmed at his progress.

When we arrived, Rachel was sitting on the bed and holding Charlie's hand. It was truly amazing. Most of the tubes where missing, and when he saw us he extended his hand, a little weak, but there we were shaking hands when just a few days ago we thought he would no longer be with us.

It was time for rejoicing. I was wishing I'd brought the ring and had it in my pocket to give to Barcelona to complete this joyful day.

Chapter Fifty

Tuesday

When I got home I called the Chief and gave him the information on Charlie. He was as surprised as the rest of us. He wanted to know when we would be able to question Charlie about the hit-and-run that almost took his life. I told him I would call my sister later that afternoon. I knew by then she would be on duty.

"Just as soon as I find out anything, Chief, I'll call you back. Is there any time in the next few days you won't be available?"

"Yea, the next three mornings I'll be working on a new case with the family of the victim. Outside of that, if I know ahead I can schedule the time for Mr. Long."

I hung up the phone and called Kim Suzuki. Still no answer. Then I called the restaurant where I was taking Barcelona for the engagement thing, and made the arrangements for the next evening. When I was through I called the florist, ordering the bouquet of flowers to be sent to the restaurant with my special instructions.

Wednesday

I picked up Barcelona at around 11:30. We were going to spend all day together. I just loved those

191

Wednesdays when we had the whole day to ourselves, to do whatever we wanted, with no time schedule.

We started out the day with a late breakfast, then went to see Charlie Long's movie that had just come out. It was playing at one of the new movie theaters, and because of the hit-and-run, and all the news about the murders and attempted murders, the movie house was packed. We both agreed that the movie would have been successful even if there was no publicity about Charlie.

It was a great movie and he was very good. We could see why his pictures were all money-makers. Apart from being so handsome he was also a remarkable actor. We left the theater admiring his talent, and Barcelona said she was still hoping that Charlie would be able to make the movie with her. It wasn't scheduled until the next year to begin shooting. And now with his amazing recovering, we both had high hopes that it would be possible.

We shopped at the big mall that was just a few blocks away, because Barcelona said there were some things she wanted to buy. After we were through, I told her of my dinner plans.

She was excited, and asked, "Why are we going to such a fancy place?" She knew I didn't like to get all dressed up. She added, "Sam, what is the special occasion. I'm getting very curious?"

"Well, I suppose I'm going to have to get used to it. After we get married I know there will be times I'll have to go to places like this with you. But for now I'm taking you home so you can rest for awhile, then you can do all the things women do when they're going out on the town. I'll pick you up at seven-thirty. Our reservations are at eight."

I completely ignored her question about the big occasion. I had made special arrangements for dinner at the Glace Restaurant. They specialized in steak and lobster, which was Barcelona's favorite, but they also had many other delicacies on the menu. It was very elegant: suits and ties for the men and evening apparel for the ladies. It was the place where movie stars and theater stars went while in New York. I had been there once, for my sister and her husband's five year anniversary. The food was great, but too fancy for me.

But for the night that I would become engaged, I thought it would be the perfect place. After all, the most famous person on Broadway at that time would be on my arm as we walked in.

I had taken my suit out of the closet on Monday to make sure it would still fit. It did, so I took it to the cleaners to be cleaned and pressed, along with my shirt, and then took my shoes to be polished. I was ready to go.

I tried to rest for awhile but was too anxious to leave, so I showered and shaved and just before I got dressed I called Kim Suzuki again. Still no answer.

The time had come for me to pick up Barcelona. She looked absolutely beautiful. I had to swallow hard from keeping the lump in my throat from coming out. Her blonde hair was tossed around her face very much like Rita Hayworth in the movie *Gilda*. The dress was deep purple and it looked like satin. It definitely showed off her figure. The top was off the shoulders, and glistened down to her waist. Her shoes matched the dress. She told me later she had them dyed.

When she came out of her building, the taxi driver gave out a long whistle and asked, "Is she waiting for you, or are you dreaming as I am?"

I said nothing. When the taxi stopped I got out and assisted Barcelona into the back of the cab. Then I ran over to the other side behind the driver's seat. As I did, I heard the cabbie say, "You are sure one lucky guy!"

His window was rolled down, and I whispered back to him, "I know."

I told Barcelona how beautiful she looked, and she responded with a thank you and a kiss, and said that I looked very handsome.

I had made plans with the maitre d' beforehand, and was praying all would work out as planned. While he led us to our table, I felt like the whole room was looking at who I thought was the most beautiful woman there. As we came in, the band was playing our song. Not that we had one, but it became our love song after that night. It was called *Little Things Mean a Lot*. Some of you may remember it.

We ordered our dinner and I ordered a bottle of champagne. Barcelona said that she didn't think I drank. I told her I didn't, but this was a very, very, special occasion.

She just smiled, but didn't ask any questions. By this time I was pretty sure she knew what was going on.

Right on time the waiter brought over a beautiful arrangement of one dozen white roses with a red rose in the middle. Tied to the red rose was the heart-shaped box with the red embossed rose and a short note I had written. *My heart will always be yours . . . love you, Sam.*

As she reached for the box, moisture began to blur her eyes, and as she read the note a tear rolled down each side of her face. She untied the box from the red rose's stem and handed it to me as she wiped away the tears that were now coming out profusely. I opened the box facing her, and said, "Barcelona Jones, love of my life, will you marry me and become my wife?"

I felt like the whole room was not only watching us, but was waiting for her reply. Then because of the tears and little sobs that were coming from her, all she could do was nod her head. I took the ring out of the box and walked around the table where I took her hand, knelt down on one knee and placed the ring on her left hand ring finger. I looked up at her and she finally said, "Yes, of course I'll marry you."

I stood up, leaned over, kissed her, and said, "Thank you."

With that, the dinner guests began to applaud. The orchestra started to play and I led Barcelona Jones, soon to be my wife, to the dance floor.

Chapter Fifty-One

The evening could not have been more perfect. Many people came by our table and congratulated us. We laughed, talked about our future together and had a great time. Barcelona even started to plan the wedding, and wondered if my parents would consent to having the wedding and the reception at their home. She said while she was there at their going-away party, she thought how beautiful the house and grounds were, and that it would be a perfect place for a wedding. I assured her that Mom and Dad would be honored to have it there, if that was what she wanted.

Just before we left, Barcelona said she'd call for a news conference in the morning to give the details to the press. She said she was happy to hold it, because it meant we didn't have to keep our relationship a secret any longer. She also mentioned that there might be someone who was there that night in the restaurant, who had witness my proposal, who might tell the press before she could, but that was all right with her. She would give the press the true information on our wedding plans and our engagement when she met with them.

On the way home I asked her if she had seen Kim Suzuki. She said she hadn't seen him since Sunday night's performance. The understudy had taken over for the last two performances. It wasn't too unusual, as the part was very small and the director didn't seem to mind.

"Why do you ask, Sam?"

"I've been trying to get a hold of him. I called him a few times but got no answer, so I was just curious."

"You don't think anything has happened to him?"

I told her no, but I did wonder: not that something might have happened to Kim Suzuki but maybe he was involved somehow with the murders. And because he'd disappeared after our interview, I thought maybe we were getting too close.

I made a mental note to call the law firm he had been working for in the morning, to see if they had seen him or knew of his whereabouts.

I hated to see our evening come to a close, but like all good things it had to happen. I asked Barcelona if she wanted me to go to the press conference with her. She said, "Yes, that would be nice, Sam. That way, everyone can see how handsome my future husband is!"

Barcelona warned me that there would be many pictures taken for the papers and magazines. She told me she'd call in the morning to let me know the time. She admitted she wasn't looking forward to all the questions, especially the personal ones.

We walked for awhile and then hailed a taxi. When we arrived at Barcelona's place we said our goodbyes. She looked at the ring and again said how beautiful it was and that she couldn't have been more happy with anything else. She was surprised that I had designed it, saying it made it more special and that through the years she would probably find out more specials things about me.

We again told each other of our love, and as I walked away to get into the cab I looked back at her. She was smiling and looking down at her left-hand ring finger. We waved to each other, and as I got into the taxi the lump in my throat got bigger and the tears rolled down my face. I didn't care if the driver saw me or not. My thoughts were on Barcelona and how much I loved her.

Chapter Fifty-Two

Thursday

The next morning when I woke up I was thinking about Kim Suzuki. I would have bet my life on his innocence in the Broadway murders. The thought came to me again to call the firm of lawyers, Bradley and Sons, and see if they had heard from him. Before I did that I called Kim Suzuki at home one more time, but still no answer.

I looked up the phone number of the law firm and they answered immediately.

"Hi, this is Sam Jones. I'm wondering if I could speak to one of the Bradleys?"

"Certainly. Are you Sam Jones, the detective?"

I smiled to myself and said, "Yes I am."

"One moment please, Mr. Jones."

"Mr. Sam Jones, this is Bradley Senior. I'm so glad you called. Our firm has been wanting to contact you to see if you would be available work on some of our cases. We might need someone like you to help us investigate on behalf of our clients. How can I help you?"

"Well, thanks. Just give us a call anytime, and if I'm available I'd be happy to help anyway I can. The reason I'm calling is to see if you know the whereabouts of Kim Suzuki? He told us that he was helping you out on a case of some kind, although of course he never told us what it was. I'm trying to locate him."

"Kim is a great go-getter and does an excellent job for us. This is the second time we've used him. Right now he's on an assignment for us in California. He checks back every evening, so I know he's okay. Would you like to have him call you? He'll be returning early this afternoon."

"No, that won't be necessary. In fact, I'd prefer that you didn't mention this call to him."

"Of course. He's not in any kind of trouble is he? If so, our firm would represent him free of charge. That's how much we think of him."

"No, no trouble. I might have a job for him when he's through working for you. He said something about finishing the assignment you gave him by the tenth of next month. I can wait."

"You'll enjoy working with him. I recommend him highly. Our personal investigator is doing a job for us in Tokyo, which is why we needed Kim."

"Thanks. I can tell you're very happy with him and his work."

We said our goodbyes and I knew for sure I wanted Kim Suzuki working for me ... exclusively.

I waited for the afternoon to call my sister as I knew by then Erica would be through with her rounds with her patients. I checked to see if the Chief and I could come in and ask Charlie Long some questions about the hit-and-run accident.

She said she'd check with him to see if he was okay about seeing us, and call back and let me know. She also congratulated me on my engagement. She said she was so happy after reading the letter that I had sent to our folks. I told her that tomorrow afternoon, or Saturday, would be good for the Chief, if it was all right with Charlie.

About an hour later Erica called saying that Saturday afternoon around 1:30 at the hospital would be good. I called Marty and he said he'd be there.

I picked the phone back up and dialed Barcelona. I was curious to know what was happening with the media interview. She said she was just going to call me and tell me she decided not to do it that way and make such a big deal out of it. She called *Photoplay Magazine* and spoke to a reporter there who had always been good to her, and told him about our engagement. He was coming by to pick up a picture of the two of us that had been taken the night before at the restaurant. She was delighted that she didn't have to worry about all the questions that would have been asked by all the news reporters. "After all, I'm not one of those famous movies stars from Hollywood."

I said, "Not yet, my love. Not yet."

Chapter Fifty-Three

Friday

Another day had gone by without seeing Barcelona, and I wanted to see her on Friday. The weekend was coming upon us, and that meant I wouldn't get to see much of her then. So before I went to bed on Thursday night I called her and we made arrangements to have breakfast and spend the rest of the day together. The two choices were the zoo or Coney Island. Since the zoo was a little closer we decided to go there.

On the way to breakfast, Barcelona brought up the subject of Brenda Summers and asked what my feelings were about her. I mentioned her strange entry into the office and her acting ability and how she had the Chief and me fooled, and how he wasn't too happy about the whole thing.

"You mean she really did that, Sam? We joked about it and I said I thought you might find it humorous, but I didn't think she'd really *do* it. I told you she was a strange bird, but I love her anyway."

I wondered if Brenda thought the little episode in my office would change our minds about her, by trying to make us think that she was a special friend of the Star.

CHUCK ANTONE JR.

I reminded Barcelona again that friends do commit murder, especially jealous ones. Barcelona was not biting it, and said, "Come on, Sam, Brenda may be capable of doing many strange things ... but not murder. I still think you're barking up the wrong tree."

"I hope so, for your sake. But being in this business for as long as I have, nothing surprises me anymore. Please don't say anything to anyone, but Brenda *is* one of our prime suspects. Be careful and always be on guard when you're with her. It's best not to tell her things like where you're going and what time you'll be somewhere, especially telling her when you'll be alone. For instance, she made the Chief and me believe that you were the one who suggested the acting bit she did. And another thing. We're wondering why no one else has come forward to say that they saw this mysterious man that Brenda claims she saw."

"Sorry, Sam, I still can't believe Brenda's involved in the killings and that she's the one who pushed me into the bus. But for your peace of mind I promise I'll be very careful."

The day went much too quickly, and when I returned home there was a message for me on the machine. I played it.

"Hi, Mr. Jones, this is Kim Suzuki. I was wondering if you located my job application, and if so, what your thoughts on it were. If I don't hear from you in a couple of days I'll call back and bring you a new one if you like."

Since it was still early I gave Kim a call back. I made arrangements for him to come into the office the next morning and told him I had an assignment for him if he was interested. He must have thanked me a least a dozen times and asked if it was just a onetime offer. I said "We'll talk about it tomorrow when you get here."

By his voice and the many thanks I could tell he was elated to have the opportunity to show me what he could do.

When I made the appointment I also remembered that the Chief and I were going to the hospital to talk to Charlie Long at 1:30. We were hoping he could tell us if the driver of the car that hit him was male or female. Maybe he saw the mysterious man who might or might not be the figment of Brenda Summers' mind.

By now it was getting late so I went to bed and replayed the day in my mind with my now-fiancée, Barcelona Jones, stage actress and soon to be a famous Hollywood movie star.

Chapter Fifty-Four

Saturday

Kim Suzuki arrived fifteen minutes early, which was something else I liked about him. He was very excited and thanked me yet again for giving him a chance to show what he could do. He asked me what I thought of his qualifications and his job request. I told him I was impressed by it. A big smile came over his face: not an overly proud smile but a happy one.

"Mr. Jones, what are my chances of coming and working for you permanently?"

"I'd say the chances are pretty good, Kim. Of course, we need to come to some kind of a salary agreement and what kind of hours you can put into any assignments I give you. I was thinking when you get through with the Bradley job, I believe in about two more weeks——"

Before I could finish, he said, "I'm through with that job. I gave them my final report yesterday, two weeks ahead of time. And my time with the play can also be terminated at short notice. So I could work for you full time immediately, Mr. Jones. My salary doesn't have to be big at the start, and my time is yours at least for the next eight months. Then I'll be getting married and would like some time off for our honeymoon. After that, I would need more stable hours. Until then, I'm all yours."

"Slow down, my friend. I'll come up with some proposal and give it to you. I want you to be honest with me how you feel about the offer. If we're to work together, honesty must be a factor in our relationship. Please read it carefully and then get back to me. Until then, I do have a job for you, if you want to give it a go."

I handed him a piece of paper that I'd written three names on, along with some information on each person on the list.

He looked it over. "Wow, this is great. When do you want the information, and which one do you want me to start on first?"

"That's up to you. I just want you to bring me back the information on any one of them. The choice is yours. Pick anyone you like."

He smiled, as if to say, "I know you're trying to find out what kind of work I can do by tracking down one of these people."

He was clearly even smarter than I thought. I waited to see what he'd say next.

"I'm on it, Mr. Jones. I'll have all the information for you in less than seventy-two hours."

Two of the names I'd given him were suspects, each one having a connection with the murders. But the third and last name I just picked out at random, as I wanted to give him three names. I was sort of testing him to see what he would come up with.

He shook my hand. "I'll be looking forward to reading what your offer will be for the job. I know you'll be fair. So don't worry, Mr. Jones, I'm sure I'll be able to accept whatever you offer. You're one person I've been praying about working for."

I arrived at the hospital around 1:15 and waited for the Chief. I didn't go straight up to see Charlie Long, because I felt he might start giving me some information, and I wanted to wait for Marty. I thought that was fair and I was sure he would appreciate it.

Just after 1:40 the Chief came briskly walking up to me. "Sorry I'm late, but I got caught in traffic. Thanks for waiting for me. I knew you would. You're so much like your father. *Integrity* should be plastered on your office door in big bold letters."

We met Erica in the hallway and she said that he was waiting for us. When we opened his door and walked in it was like looking at a miracle. The Hollywood star's color was back and there was a big smile on his face. We didn't need to be detectives to tell he had just showered – his hair was still wet. He was shaved and looking great.

Rachel, his wife, greeted us with a warm welcome and then excused herself. Charlie explained that she didn't want to hear the gory details about the accident again.

"Charlie, you look great. Many prayers have been answered." I shook his hand and then introduced him to the Chief.

"Thanks, Mr. Long, for agreeing to see us this afternoon. I was here the day of the accident but you were in a coma, so I'm sure you don't remember me. I'm happy to see you doing so well. You have certainly recovered remarkably quickly."

"Thanks, Chief. Please feel free to ask whatever you wish. I don't know how much help I can be, as I don't remember a lot that happened that night."

"What do you remember, Mr. Long? Did you notice the make of the car? Or if it was a man or woman driving? Anything will help us, no matter how small you think it is."

"Well, I remember leaving the hotel. I wanted to get out in the fresh air and walk a little. I'd asked my new agent Edward to go with me, but he declined. I walked out of the hotel, looked back and waved to him. He was standing by the lighted window. It was getting dark now. I crossed the street and saw this car was coming speeding towards me. The car's lights weren't on. I do remember that."

"And the make of car?" the Chief asked.

He shook his head. "I'm not too good on cars. It was large. Long hood. Maybe a few years old. Dark blue or black probably."

"And the driver?"

"Sorry, Chief, I couldn't tell for sure if a male or a female was driving. But it looked like an older person, wearing a hat and coat and with a funny looking smile. I felt the car hit my body, felt a sharp pain, and then I must have blacked out. That's about it. I've been lying here trying to come up with something more, but that's all I can remember."

"What do you mean when you say a funny smile, Charlie?"

'I'm not sure, Sam. It happened so fast. I think it was something to do with his upper front teeth. I think they were missing. Sorry, wish I could be more help."

"Actually, Mr. Long, you've been a big help to us. Thanks for letting us come in and talk to you."

We talked for a little while, then the Chief and I left. We told Charlie we didn't want to tire him out. He

212

said he was fine and that we didn't have to leave. By that time Rachel had returned, so we left them alone.

When we got outside, the Chief said, "Well, it looks like Brenda Summers *did* see a man."

"Yes, or the mysterious man is Brenda Summers herself. Remember, she's an actress and a very good one. She most likely has access to all the props at the theater. Wig, hat, coat and so on. The only thing that puzzles me is the two missing teeth. But I guess make-up of some kind could take care of that too." I stopped and held onto the Chief arm. "No, that can't be so. Brenda Summers said that the person in the theater ran their tongue through the gap – assuming she's telling the truth."

The Chief smiled. "Good thinking, Sam. You could still be right about the make-up. If the driver *was* Brenda Summers, she wouldn't have needed a real gap when driving the car. Just black paint on her front teeth, so let's still treat her as a major suspect."

Chapter Fifty-Five

Monday

I talked to Barcelona briefly on the phone on Sunday when she called to say everyone loved her ring and was wondering where I got it. She also said that most of the people there at the theater couldn't believe I'd designed it.

Monday morning I went to the office early. Tooth gap or no tooth gap, I was still in the dark about who was the murderer. Again and again I went over my notes, looking for something I might have missed. I called the Chief and discovered that he too was puzzled. We had a couple suspects but still nothing firm, nothing where we could say, "That's it. We have enough evidence to arrest someone."

He mentioned again that maybe there was someone else we hadn't thought of. He suggested that perhaps we should call the cast and crew together one more time. I told him I'd talk to Barcelona to see if she could arrange it for us.

"Barcelona Jones." The Chief said the name slowly. He sighed. "Do you think, Sam, that maybe *she* has something to do with the murders? She could have thrown herself in front of that bus at just the right time, making sure she wouldn't get badly hurt?"

"Definitely not, Chief. You see, I got myself engaged about five days ago and——"

Before I could finish, the Chief interrupted me. "*Engaged?* Wow you work fast. Don't keep me in suspense any longer. Which one is she?"

I knew he'd not read *Photoplay*. It wasn't his thing. "Would you believe the star, Barcelona Jones?"

"Come on, Sam, no joking around. Confess up. Who's the lady who's knocked you off your feet?"

"I just did, Chief."

"You did? I didn't hear any name. Just Barcelona Jones..." Then silence. "You've got to be kidding. It can't be."

"Yep, it sure is. The love of my life is the star of *Murder on Broadway*. Barcelona Jones herself."

"I still don't believe it. Are you pulling my leg or are you serious?"

"I couldn't be more serious. It truly is her."

"When's the wedding? This is one I'm surly not going to miss. I will be invited, won't I?"

"Not sure yet when the wedding will be, but of course you'll be on the list. One of the first to be invited."

I hung up the phone and started to get a little melancholy. The Chief was actually the first person outside the family I'd told. Before the tears could swell up, the phone rang. It was Kim Suzuki. He said he had all the information that I'd requested.

"You're mighty quick, Kim. It's been less than forty-eight hours. Who did you chose to investigate?"

"I wasn't sure which one, so I picked the last name on your list."

I was a little disappointed, because I'd written

that name down simply to give Kim three names, to test his skills.

"If you're not too busy, come by the office. You can give me the information you've gathered and we can talk about you coming and working for me full time and exclusively."

I wasn't sure how he would to react to full time and exclusive, but his reaction was overwhelming.

"Full time and exclusive? *Just* what I was looking for. I'm excited. I'll be right in and sign the agreement, if that's necessary."

"I'll be waiting for you, and there will be no agreement signing. That *won't* be necessary."

When I told Donna about Kim, she was elated and could hardly wait for him to start. When he arrived, Donna personally brought Kim into my office and fiddled around listening to all that I was telling him.

Before I started, Kim handed me the information he had acquired. I laid it on my desk and explained what I would expect if he agreed to work for me. I mentioned a starting salary and the days he would need to come into the office, even if there was no searching to do.

I told him he could use my old office, since I had taken over my dad's when he retired. I would also furnish him with a desk, a typewriter, his own phone line, and whatever else he might need pertaining to the job.

"The room needs some cleaning, and the files will need rearranging, and so on. But you can do it at your leisure. Donna will help you."

"When do I start? I'm ready right now, if you're willing. And I have my own portable typewriter I can bring in, so no need to furnish me one."

"Don't you want to think about it first?"

"Why? This is what I've been waiting for. My own office, the perfect boss and a cute secretary."

He looked over and winked at Donna. She was in seventh heaven. She gave me that look like, *Don't let this one get away.*

"Okay, then start whenever you want," and with those words from me, Kim went into his new office. It had become part of a storage room for old files that we no longer needed. Donna had said many times, "Boss, we've got to clean that room some day. You may want to hire somebody to help you."

Kim looked around. "This is perfect. Can I paint it and use my creativity to make it my own?"

"It's all yours, Kim. Do whatever you want with it."

Donna said, "If you need anything, just ask. I'll help you as much as I can. But first let's get rid of all those old files."

I went over to my desk with a smile on my face, sat down and opened up the investigation folder Kim had brought. My smile soon turned to a frown and then bewilderment. I called Kim in. "Are you sure of all this information?"

"One hundred percent. Is it all right?

"I'll say it is. You have just helped us find the killer and solve the case of *Murder on Broadway.*"

Chapter Fifty-Six

I immediately dialed the Chief at the station. I felt pretty sure he would be there.

"Chief Mead speaking."

"Hi, Chief, this is Sam. I have some great news for you. Can you come over to my office?"

"I suppose you don't want to give it to me on the phone, right?"

"That's right. I think it would be better to hand you the information myself … It's a killer."

I had to smile at myself for the remark.

"Give me about an hour and I'll be there. Is that soon enough for you?"

"Well, the sooner the better."

I hung up the phone and read the file over and over. It was still hard for me to believe.

Marty arrived within forty-five minutes.

"What's this killer news you have for me?"

I handed him the file. He opened it up and began to read. I watched the look on his face. His expression I'm sure was about the same as mine when I read what Kim had come up with. He put the folder down. I could tell he was deep in thought.

"I have an idea, Sam. Let's call all three here to

your office. Make up something, anything, but don't tell them that anyone else will be here. How about tomorrow morning, at say around eleven? Maybe tell them we want them here because we're going to disclose to them in confidence who the killer is."

"It sounds all right with me. Is it okay if I invite Kim Suzuki and Barcelona to join us?"

"Of course. This is going to be exciting. I can't wait to see their faces. Especially the face of the murderer."

After he left, I called Barcelona and told her our plan to meet at 11:00 in the morning with the three who were on my list. I gave her no other information, cautioning her to tell no one else about the meeting. I was also getting excited to meet with the three, and to finally close the case.

Chapter Fifty-Seven

Tuesday
The next day, the Chief arrived fifteen minutes after Barcelona. He congratulated her on our upcoming marriage and said I was sure a lucky guy. Then turning to me with his mischievous grin, he said, "Another beauty and the beast story!"

All three of us laughed, knowing the inside joke of how, when I was in school, many called me and my sister that – of course, Erica being the beauty.

When all three arrived, we sat down in an informal group that Kim had arranged. They were surprised to see the others there. We sat in a circle facing each other so we could look at each others' faces.

When everyone was comfortable, we announced to all that we had found the killer and that it was one of them. They gasped and looked at each other with disbelief. The three on my list were John Ashland the lead actor, Mike Larson the agent, and Brenda Summers, the actor of many parts.

Brenda looked over at Kim. "I know it's not you, Kim. You're too sweet a kid to do something like that."

"Thanks, Miss Summers. You've always been very nice to me."

Mike the agent said, "Well I know it's not me, and it seems that Kim here is too nice of a guy, so that leaves Miss Summers and Mr. Ashton – and the star herself. Barcelona. Which one is it?"

"Wait a minute," John Ashland broke in angrily. "Let's not completely leave Kim out of it. He's the one who pulled the trigger. Besides, you're not out of the running yet either, Mike. You were their agent. And what about that strange man Brenda said she saw. Where is he?"

The Chief broke in, "Well actually, that person is here. The so-called strange man is one of you."

All three looked around at each other.

"Whoever this mysterious man or woman is…" with that, the Chief looked over at Summers and then continued, "…had access to all the props at the theater. Anybody could have walked in and made themselves at home, picking and choosing whatever they wanted."

Suddenly the office door opened and in walked the mysterious man.

Brenda Summers shouted out, *"That's him. That's him!"*

The two others started asking questions, and mass confusion began.

I waited for a few moments until everyone stopped shouting out and settled down. Then I said, "No, this isn't mysterious man. It's someone dressed to look like him."

When I said that, Donna straightened up, took off the hat and gloves and smiled very quickly, revealing two missing teeth.

"I can't believe she's the killer," John Ashland shouted.

"No, this isn't the killer. This is my secretary, Donna. We found the coat and hat at the theater. It may or may not be the original that was worn by the mysterious person, but very close. With the help of the makeup department it looks like her two front teeth are missing."

Brenda Summers shouted out, "But I'm very sure that the man I saw *really* had his two front teeth missing. Like I said, he put his tongue through the opening, making sure I saw that his teeth weren't there."

Each one by now was looking at each other and giving big smiles to show they had all their teeth.

"Yes, that's correct. The killer's teeth are really missing. We checked with their dentist and one of you has two false teeth right in front."

Two of them looked around at each other, but one was staring at the floor. They waited, but there was no response. Then all of a sudden it sunk in who the true killer was.

Chapter Fifty-Eight

Mike Larson shook his head, saying that is wasn't possible that the person not looking up at them was the killer. He reminded us that the man was in the hospital the day Anthony Sparks was shot. Someone had slipped peanut extract into his food that day, which is why he wasn't at that evening performance.

The Chief replied, "No, we *thought* he was in the hospital. Sam and I forgot to check what time he was admitted. John Ashland called the hospital in the afternoon saying he was coming in, but he didn't check in until six forty-five that evening. It seems he ministered his own peanut extract into his body and knew just the right amount to give himself. We all thought he was going to die, and that someone else slipped the stuff into his food. We felt so sorry for him thinking he was a victim, and we stupidly didn't think of him as a villain. We just didn't do our job. Kim, who now works for Sam, found out some important evidence from Ashland's dentist."

By now, Mike Larson and Brenda Summers were sitting on the edge of their seats.

The Chief said, "You guessed it. His two front teeth are missing. The teeth you see when he smiles are false. He got rid of Anthony Sparks by changing the bullets to live rounds, so he would have one less competitor for the movie roll. He also found the fugu poison that killed Peter Holmes. How, I don't know yet. And then he tried to kill Miss Jones and Charlie Long."

Silence filled the room and Ashland didn't deny it. All he said was, "I want a lawyer. I deserved the movie roll. I'm a greater actor, and getting rid of the two I killed was easy. I had a hunch that Barcelona, the so-called *star* of the show would choose Charlie Long for the movie roll. When I didn't succeed in getting rid of her, my next choice was that Long fellow from Hollywood. The part belongs to the best actor … and that's me."

When he was through, the door to Kim's new office opened and two policemen came out. The Chief said, "John Ashland, you are under arrest for the murders of Anthony Sparks, Peter Homes, and the attempted murders of Charlie Long and Barcelona Jones the true *star* of *Murder on Broadway.*" He emphasized the word *"star."*

Then turning to his police officers, he said, "Take him down to the station and book him. On the way, make sure you read him the Miranda rights."

Barcelona finally spoke up. She'd been quiet all through the session, "I can't believe it. I can't believe that John is the person who tried to kill me by pushing me in front of that bus."

"I can," Brenda blurted out. "I had a hunch it might be him. I've never liked him. He was a sneaky…" then she paused. "Well, you can finish the sentence."

Chapter Fifty-Nine

Well, my friends, that's how I met Barcelona Jones, stage and screen actress. We've had a great life together. Our wedding took place at my folks' home. They had the house and backyard beautifully decorated. Around the pool were tables and chairs, and on the lawn area one huge tent that sat around one hundred and seventy-five people. We had over two hundred who attended our special day, not counting the press. It was a sunset wedding and the weather couldn't have been better.

We took a cruise for our honeymoon to Spain and Portugal. We loved it so much that we returned five years later. It was on that trip our daughter, Lisbon, was conceived.

Barcelona made the movie version of *Murder on Broadway* with Charlie Long. It was a box office success, bringing in big bucks to the delight of the producers and director. Barcelona and Charlie won Academy awards, plus it won the Oscar for best picture.

Barcelona also won the Tony for her performance on Broadway, as did Brenda Summers, who is now part of our family. I get a big kick out of her honesty and blunt remarks. When in a conversation with her, she holds nothing back. As Barcelona has said many times, "Either you like her or you don't."

After three years of marriage, Sam Jr. came along, and right after that my folks decided to sell the house and move into a retirement community. We bought the house and have lived there for over forty-five years. When we decide to move out, Sam Jr. will move in with his family. Our other two kids are in agreement with that.

Barcelona's grandmother came to live with us. She loved the kids, and babysat often when Barcelona and I needed a break. Barcelona went on to make more movies, all which were successful, but her heart was always for the Broadway stage. She had said so often, "I love to act in front of a live audience."

Soon after all three of the children arrived, she semi-retired and then eventually didn't go back until all of our kids were grown. When she did return to Broadway, she took it by storm, winning a couple of more Tony Award's, one again for the revival of *Murder on Broadway*.

Wow, it's getting late so I must go to be with Barcelona. I can't believe we'll be celebrating our fiftieth year together as husband and wife. My, how time goes by.

The little church I attended has become our little church, and whenever we can, we attend. The pastor and his wife are still there, and have become very good friends of ours. He is of course retired now, but he still preaches on special occasions, and he officiated at our marriage ceremony. All five of us have been baptized by him over the years.

Sorry, but I really have to go. I don't want to be late. And I have to make one stop on the way.

Epilogue
Chapter Sixty

Sam ran out the door, not wanting to be late. The one stop he had to make before meeting Barcelona was the flower shop. He had already placed the order ... one dozen white roses and one red rose. He gave specific instructions as always for the red rose to be placed in the middle of the arrangement. There would be no card this time. He would be telling her in person how much he loved her.

He arrived just in time. He knew she would be waiting for him. Carrying the flower arrangement in both hands he used his shoulder to open the door. It was heavy but he managed to swing it open. The room was filled with flowers of congratulations, each one having a card with encouraging words for their fifty years together.

Barcelona smiled at Sam as she saw the beautiful white roses, and the red one in the middle. It was just what she had been waiting for as Sam entered her hospital room. He had to swallow hard to hold back his tears as he looked over at his wife. She still seemed as beautiful to him as the first day he met her in that taxi, even though she had lost so much weight, and most of her hair had fallen out. The wig he had bought her a week ago had cheered her up, and she had gotten a big laugh over it. Today one of the nurses had to help her put it on as she was too weak to do it herself. She had been waiting for her one true love to arrive, and wanted to look her best for him.

They both knew the time was near when she would no longer be part of his life on this earth. Sam walked over to the bed, took her hand in his and leaned over and kissed her first on the forehead then on the lips. This was a custom he had started many years ago. How and why, he didn't know. It just seemed to come naturally.

Barcelona motioned for him to sit on the bed close to her. Looking up at him and in a weak voice that was almost a whisper, she said, "I love you, my beloved Sam."

Sam was unable to control his emotions, even though he had promised himself he would. The tears filled his eyes, then freely ran from his eyes to his cheeks and on to the sheet that covered Barcelona.

"Be brave, Sam. Remember what we learned at our little church where God said, "There is a time to weep and a time to laugh. We've been so blessed that there has been more laughing then weeping in our lifetime together."

Holding hands they shared those happy times. Reminiscing over the past fifty years, remembering how they first met, the zoo and Coney Island, the fun they had trying to ring the monkey's mouth, and now their three children and how much the Lord had blessed them all through the years.

For a few moments, silence fell over the room, both of them in their own secret thoughts. Sam's of course was how much he would miss Barcelona, wondering how he could live without her.

Finally Barcelona spoke up, her voice barely heard. "I'm getting tired, Sam. I need to rest for a little while. I think you've worn me out." There was a slight smile on her face.

"Of course, my love. I should have thought of that. I'll go over there and sit while you rest." Sam pointed to the only chair in the private room.

"No, please go out and get some fresh air, or go to the hospital cafeteria and get something to eat. Or at least have a cup of coffee while I rest. I'll be just fine."

Sam was thinking how brave his wife was, and was wondering if he was in that bed instead of her, would he be doing as well?

"No, I'm staying right here with you. Besides, I've ordered a very special dinner for us tonight to celebrate. Even two glasses of champagne. You rest. I've brought a book to read, and I'll be right here when you wake up."

He got up, kissed her on the forehead and then on the lips. With tears streaming down his face, he said, "I love you, Barcelona Jones. I've always loved you from the first moment I saw you in that taxi, and I've loved you ever since."

Sam got off the bed, leaned over and kissed his wife again. He held onto her hand, not wanting to let it go.

Barcelona smiled at him as if to say, "You've got to let go, Sam." She gently removed her hand from his, releasing him to leave her alone for a time.

As much as Sam tried to read, he couldn't focus on the story. Every few minutes he looked over at his wife, checking to see if she was still breathing. He didn't want to let her go – even though he was sure she would be in a better place, and her pain and suffering would leave her. He knew he was being selfish, but when her time came he knew that a part of him would be leaving too.

He laid his head back on the chair and began to pray.

Chapter Sixty-One

When Sam finished praying, he again looked over at his beloved, checking the monitor to see if she was still breathing. With everything looking good he moved the chair next to Barcelona's bed. She looked so fragile, but yet peaceful. Her hand was by her side and out of the covers.

He laid his hand over hers. It seemed comforting to him. He then rested his head back on the chair and soon fell asleep.

He woke up hearing the voice of his beloved as it was straining to speak, "Sam, Sam!"

"I'm right here, my love."

"I believe it is time. Please call the children."

Sam knew exactly what she meant, and he had dreaded this moment. He had made arrangements with the oldest son, Sam Jr., that when it was their mother's time, he would call him and then he in return would call Lisbon and Jackson. They would be waiting for the final call and would drop everything and would be at the hospital as quickly as they could.

After Sam made the call he went over and sat on the bed, and again held Barcelona's hand.

She was taking deep breaths. He knew she would

hang on to her life until the children arrived – just as she had hung on so they could celebrate their fiftieth anniversary, even though the doctors said it was almost impossible.

It didn't take long. Within half an hour all three arrived. Lisbon was first, then the two boys came within minutes apart. When everyone was there and the small talk was over, Barcelona said, "Let's hold hands and pray. There are things I want to thank the Lord for."

The five of them stood around the bed holding hands, with tears flowing freely from their eyes. No one could speak except for Barcelona.

Barcelona took a deep breath, trying to speak louder so all could hear. "Dear Lord, I want to thank you for my family. I've been so blessed by each one of them and their families. You, Lord, have been very good to me. I ask that you would bless them all the days of their lives, and you will always be the center of their lives and their protector."

She had to pause in her prayer, to get her strength to carry on. Then she said, "Please bless their wives and husbands and my grandchildren, that they will grow up knowing you in a personal way. I pray that they will have the marriage that Sam and I have had all of these years, filled with love and respect and much joy. Thank you for Sam, Lord. You couldn't have chosen a better mate for me. I ask that you will watch over him, giving him your strength and helping him to go on with his life knowing I am free from pain and in the presence of you, Lord. And believing that someday we will be together again … Amen."

They all wiped away their tears, repeating the word "Amen"

"Now," Barcelona continued faintly, "I want the three of you to leave for a while, so I can spend a few moments with your father."

Each one made no argument, and one by one they reached over and hugged their mother, and in their own ways said their goodbyes.

When the three of them left the room, Sam sat back in the chair and leaning over Barcelona laid his head on her chest. She put her arm around his back. It was painful for her but she wanted to do it. She wanted to hold him for what she knew would be the last time.

His tears became quiet sobs, as if he was grasping for air. "I love you, my love, and I don't want you to leave me. But I know you must. My life will never be the same without you, and part of me will go with you."

"I love you too, Sam. But please remain strong, especially for the children. We *will* meet again."

He didn't want to move, but turning his head he looked up at her. She'd also been crying.

They smiled at each other. He laid his head back on her chest and the only words that came out of his mouth were, "I love you."

"I know you do. Sam. But it's time for me to leave you. You have *always* been the love of my life."

There were a few moments of silence before Sam could respond. But before his words would come out he realized, with his head next to her heart, that it had stopped beating, He lay there for a few seconds hoping she would start breathing again, but it never happened.

He got up kissed, her on the forehead, then on the lips. And with tears streaming down his face, said, "I love you. I've always loved you from the first moment I saw you in that taxi, and I've loved you ever since, my Barcelona Jones."

Chapter Sixty-Two

Sam left the hospital room as the nurses and doctors were hurrying in. He walked down the corridor to the elevators, wiping away his tears. It was time to tell his children that their mother was now in the arms of Jesus.

When Sam entered the cafeteria his children were waiting for him. There was no need for him to explain. They could tell by the look on their father's face that their mother was no longer with them. After tight embraces and more tears they made plans to meet the next morning to make arrangements for the memorial service. Then each went their own way to be alone with their thoughts and memories of their mother. Of course Sam's thoughts would be on the love of his life.

As Sam was sitting in the taxi going home, he started to reminisce about his life with Barcelona. He would miss her for sure, but what great memories he would have – and of course the assurance that he would see her again.

A smile came over his face as he thought about the time Barcelona walked forward one Sunday morning in church to commit her life to the Lord. It was the same day he had also walked forward. He hadn't known that Barcelona was in his little church that morning, as it was a last minute decision by her to visit the little church that Sam often spoke about. She had come in late and was sitting in the back row.

The pastor's message was very powerful, challenging the congregation to surrender themselves to the Lord. When the pastor gave the altar call, Sam got up from his seat. While walking forward he wondered what Barcelona would think of him making such a commitment.

That was when he felt someone's hand in his. He looked down at the hand that he knew so well, and a big smile came over his face as he looked up and saw tears flowing from Barcelona's eyes.

Sam smiled as he remembered them holding hands as they walked forward, surrendering their lives together to the Lord. What a great moment that was for both of them. That was how he knew for sure that he and Barcelona would someday be together again.

He sat in the cab in silence, wishing that they could have had a little more time together on this earth. The tears began to flow freely again, but even with the tears profusely coming from his eyes a peace came over him.

At that moment he was sure he heard Barcelona's voice whispering in his ear. "Remember, Sam, it's better to have loved and lost than never to have loved at all."

Sam wiped away his tears, saying, "I know, my love, and I'll be looking forward to when we will meet again."

The Prayer

If you are looking for a blessing, then please continue to give your whole life to Jesus by letting all that you do glorify Him and God, our Father.

If you haven't already, please say the following prayer inviting Christ into your life. You will be glad you did.

"Dear Lord Jesus, I know I am a sinner. I believe that You are the Son of God. I believe You died for my sins and rose from the dead. I want to turn away from my sin and make You Lord of my life. I invite You to come into my life right now. Thank You, Jesus, for loving me. Amen."

If you said this prayer, have faith that Jesus came into your life immediately, as He refuses no one.

Please tell someone you know who is a Christian what you have done. And find a church and a Bible study that teaches Jesus is the way to eternal life, so God can work in you.

I also would like to hear from you.

Email: antoneyboksu@gmail.com
P.O. Box 4404, Kailua Kona, HI
96745

Mahalo,

Chuck

Made in the USA
Columbia, SC
23 May 2020

97573022R00143